Merry Ghostmas

BAKER CITY: HEARTS & HAUNTS
CHRISTMAS NOVELLA

JOSIE MALONE

MERRY GHOSTMAS
Copyright © 2023 by Josie Malone

ISBN: 979-8-88653-195-4

Published by Satin Romance
An Imprint of Melange Books, LLC
White Bear Lake, MN 55110
www.satinromance.com

Published in the United States of America.

Cover Design by Lynsee Lauritsen

PART 1

NOVEMBER 2019

CHAPTER ONE

Moises Pride drifted through the cocktail lounge at Pop's Café in Baker City, Washington. It wasn't super busy on the Wednesday night before Thanksgiving. Most people had other commitments, shopping, cooking, visiting their relatives, but he wasn't one of them, not anymore. *That's because I'm dead, dead, dead! Sorry, Momma. Another year of missing the family and your sweet potato pie.*

He spotted a few of the other ghosts hanging out, watching the action between the living patrons. An old-time holiday movie played on the big-screen TV in the corner. He floated toward the corner booth where Mayor O'Connell, a middle-aged fellow in a black suit sat talking to Zeke Garvey and Raven Driscoll-Barlow, two former soldiers who'd died in ambushes in Afghanistan. Their war might not be his, but it didn't mean they didn't have a lot in common when it came to paying the ultimate cost for serving their country. Nodding respectfully, Moises waited to join the conversation.

Raven, a thin, dark-haired wraith in camouflage fatigues and combat boots, gestured at two of the people sitting at the bar, focused on their conversation and one another. "You have something to do with that, Pride? Are you following Garvey's example and playing Cupid the way he did with Ann Barrett and Harry Colter?"

"I just gave them a little nudge." Moises followed her gaze toward the lovely ash-blonde woman in a red dress and the soldier next to her. Derek Waller was a solid, muscular man whose worn features looked as if he'd won more fights than he'd lost in his thirty-plus years of military service. A 'high and tight' style for his receding salt and pepper black hair, dark brown, almost black eyes, he was all man. "I've hung out at the barn for the past few months, and I've seen Kyra O'Neill busting her butt. She deserves someone decent, not that candy-assed horseshoer who bullies the animals when he's sure nobody's watching."

"These two were betting on how long she'd wait for some guy tonight." Raven frowned thoughtfully. "Is that him?"

"Not the Sergeant-Major," Moises said. "I already told you. She's hung up on Nick MacGillicudy and I'd like to do something about the jerk."

Mayor O'Connell rubbed his jaw. "What do you have in mind, Pride?"

"Oh, let's get in the holiday spirit." Moises pointed at the TV. "We could do our own *Christmas Carol* on Nick MacGillicudy and teach him what he needs to know."

"He might even move on and leave town," Zeke agreed. "I

never liked the guy when we were in high school. Do I get to be the *Ghost of Christmas Past*?"

"You're not the only one who has issues with Herman MacGillicudy and his son," Mayor O'Connell said. "That banker has been running Baker City into the ground for years. He tries to get his grown kids to help him rip off our kin."

"He won't be happy until he levels the place and turns it into one of his gravel pits," Zeke said. "His daughter, Dominique, the realtor may say she's on the same page, but that isn't true, not when she finds buyers for the houses and businesses here. She helped my wife purchase the bakery after I died. "

"She restores the places that need it before she sells them," Raven pointed out. "I like Dominique. She did right by my bestie and her hubby. They love the home she found for them."

The mayor nodded. "She takes after her momma, one of the O'Leary women." He paused, obviously considering Moises' suggestion. "Most of our folks will be here tomorrow when Pop sets up his holiday meal. Let's get everyone involved. Things have been downright dull since the haunted town festival last month and the Veteran's Day Parade a couple weeks ago. We need something to do now."

On Wednesday night, Thanksgiving Eve, the lounge at Pop's Café in Baker City wasn't as busy as it would be on the upcoming holiday weekend. When she'd arrived an hour ago, Kyra O'Neill had glanced around the room but didn't see her date waiting in any of the booths against the walls or at the tables in the middle of the room or playing pool in the alcove near the restrooms. He wasn't standing at the bar either. Oh no, not again! Nick MacGillicudy had a habit of being late and not showing up at all when he promised to meet her.

She sighed. For this, she'd hurried through the horse chores at work when she finished her last equitation class. She'd hustled into the barn manager apartment, nabbing the shower before her room-mate, Trina Sweeney could. Kyra turned down the offer of a microwaved pasta dinner, saying she'd eat in town with Nick. They'd arranged to meet at the café. Okay, so it was more her idea, than his, but he'd agreed. They could eat and then spend the night out at his trailer. She wasn't comfortable taking him back to the carriage house style apartment above one of the barns at Miracle Riding Stable.

Her comment earned a pitying look from the other riding instructor, but she hadn't shared the criticism both of them often heard from Nick's younger sister. She claimed he only made piecrust promises, easily made, and easily broken. When she heard about Kyra being stood up once again, Dominique would have a lot to say and none of it would be positive.

After another look around the lounge, Kyra took a deep breath and sauntered toward the bar. She'd dressed for romantic success in a cranberry red, heirloom lace dress with tight-fitting, three-quarter lace sleeves. The double-layer handkerchief hem swirled around her knees and her fashion boots tapped out a rhythm on the tile floor. She'd pinned her long ash-blonde hair into a loose bun, leaving sexy tendrils around her face, ears, and neck. Throw in the cosmetics and jewelry and she looked damned hot tonight, nothing like a 38-year-old woman who was shoveling horse pucky two hours ago.

Most of the tables appeared to be empty, not an unusual sight in Baker City. The corner booth had a cord across the end and a 'Reserved' sign hung from it. Pop MacGillicudy, the owner had said his grandfather always held the place for the mayor and his cronies. Granted, all of them had died years ago, but in this town, the ghosts were real and treated with respect. Or else!

Kyra decided she'd order a glass of white wine and wait a little longer. A somewhat successful farrier, Nick could be busy shoeing a horse for a client. She reached into her purse and drew out her cell phone. No messages. She hesitated before she texted him. She didn't want to appear desperate even if she was. She pasted on a smile and hoped it looked genuine when the bartender, Pop's daughter, Linda, a plump, brown-haired woman in a flowered shirt and black slacks approached.

There were a few years between them and way too much history, but then again Kyra knew she was too snarky to make friends easily. Sarcasm was always a good offense and defense, for that matter. She'd hitched up on a stool. "A glass of Chardonnay please."

"You look ready for the holidays." Linda smiled and reached for a goblet in the rack. The soft brown eyes warmed her pretty face. "How's life at Miracle Riding Stable? Are Debbie and her family off to eastern Washington for Thanksgiving?"

"They left early this morning." Kyra put her small red purse on the antique bar. "I'm in charge while she's gone."

"Of course you are. Debbie says she doesn't know what she'd

do without you. She's so grateful you stayed on after she bought the place last spring."

Pleasure flooded through Kyra. Granted, she often heard sincere praise from the retired Army sergeant, but it was even more special knowing the woman shared her opinion in the small town. "The housekeeper only does the daily stuff and is off for the weekend. Debbie has a special project for your cleaning company on Friday. Her grandmother is coming to visit after the holiday and Debbie hoped you'd have time to prepare the guest suite off the kitchen for her."

"No worries, as her daughters say. I'm grateful she kept me on after she hired Lupe Gonzales." Linda placed the glass on the bar. "Would you like something to eat? The kitchen's still open."

Kyra hesitated. She was supposed to have dinner with Nick, but she was hungry, close to starving. Her day started with morning chores, feeding forty equines while her boss loaded her Jeep. She and the three girls left early to meet Debbie's husband at the army base. From there, they'd head over the mountains to Pullman where Debbie's stepsons attended college.

Once they'd gone, Kyra groomed and saddled the string of lesson horses. She'd taught horsemanship classes all day and afterwards, it'd been time to muck stalls, water and feed those same horses once again. Granted, she didn't have to do it alone. Trina always did more than her share, plus they had a high school boy to help. The younger woman promised to look after the cats and dogs at Debbie's house since their boss preferred to leave the pets at home, not take them on a road trip.

"Dinner?" Linda repeated. "Dad made chicken fettuccine, and I know it's one of your favorites."

"That sounds good." Kyra lifted the glass, sipped chilled wine. "Have you seen Nick anywhere? He was going to..."

Linda froze for a moment before she picked up a damp towel to wipe the counter between them. "He hasn't been in since last night."

"We're supposed to have dinner together," Kyra said. "Everybody in town eats here at the cafe. Are you sure you haven't seen him?"

The silence grew between them. Linda reluctantly shook her head. "He was hustling some gals playing pool last night and he left with one of them. You can do so much better than my cousin's son."

Kyra nearly admitted the truth. She didn't want a different man. She wanted tall, blond, muscular Nick MacGillicudy, the raunchy, sexy man whose kisses set her on fire. She blinked hard, determined not to cry in the middle of a town where she was related to far too many of the citizenry. "Is there garlic toast to go with that pasta? Since I don't have to worry about my breath, add a couple pieces along with a small house salad. Ranch dressing on the side, please."

"You bet. I'll order your dinner right now."

Sergeant-Major Derek Waller hadn't wanted to stop on the way to Baker City from Seattle. It'd been difficult enough fighting the rush-hour, followed by the holiday traffic. He appreciated the invitation to spend the weekend and have Thanksgiving dinner with Harry Colter, one of the other sergeants from Fort Bronson, the Army Reserve base in Seattle, and his family.

Otherwise, it'd be another plastic meal at a restaurant because there was no longer a dining facility at the old historical fort that protected the city for more than a century. Now, the different units were transitioning to various sites throughout Liberty Valley and the army post would become a park. Only the military cemetery would remain at Fort Bronson along with two buildings designated as a museum.

An orphan raised in a series of foster homes, Derek enlisted as soon as he could. He'd dreaded retirement after being in the Army for more than twenty years, so he joined the Active Guard-Reserve program and was in charge of various part-time military units for another eleven years. Harry was one of the newest liaisons assigned to the post after his career in the elite Army Rangers, and their experiences in combat ensured they had a lot in common.

Parking outside Pop's Café, Derek headed into the lounge rather than the restaurant. He recognized the perky, middle-aged woman behind the bar as the owner's daughter. The tall, classy blonde in a brilliant red dress sitting on a stool at one end definitely drew his attention. He didn't know her, but he'd like to have the opportunity. He deliberately angled closer to where she sat, a nearly empty glass of white wine in front of her.

Derek eased onto the stool next to hers. "Are you ready for another one?"

"Not from someone I don't know." She turned an icy gray gaze on him. "Go away."

"I just got here." He grinned at her, entertained by the rejection. "How will you get to know me if I leave?"

"I'll handle it." She signaled the bartender. "Linda, I'm ready for my check."

"I'll have it for you in a few minutes." Linda turned her attention to Derek. "Twila Garvey dropped off those cheesecakes Ann Barrett ordered and said you'd be along to pick them up. Bad traffic, huh?"

"And a late night at the base," Derek agreed. "I barely made the PX in time to grab the case of wine her husband, Harry Colter wanted."

"I'll get those desserts. Meantime, Kyra O'Neill, play nice with others. Sergeant-Major Waller works nearly as hard as you do." Linda paused. "Have you had dinner, Derek? Or do you want Pop to throw a burger on the grill for you?"

Grateful for the half-assed introduction, Derek nodded. "Sounds good. Then I won't have to impose on Ann and Harry for a meal." After the bartender walked away, he eyed the other woman again. "So, what do you do, Kyra?"

She picked up the glass in front of her and he admired the fact that she didn't wear polish on her extremely short fingernails. He never had liked claws on women, especially red ones.

"I manage Miracle Riding Stable outside town," Kyra said. "It'd serve Linda right if I did the 'dine and dash' routine, but she'd just send half my relatives after me. And because we barely speak except at holidays, I'm not in the mood for a lecture from the likes of them."

He chuckled. "And being the perfect gentleman I am, I'd volunteer to pay for your drinks."

"I also had dinner and a piece of Twila's New York cheese-cake for dessert." Slight amusement flickered across her face, then faded. She scowled, but still looked amazing even when she was slightly pissed. "It hasn't been a good night. I shouldn't take it out on you."

"Guy's an asshat."

She blinked, shocked. "How did you know I was stood up?"

"Dump him. Anyone who'd blow off a date with you isn't worth your time or effort." He paused. "I bet you know little Princess Devon, Ann's daughter."

"She's one of my best students," Kyra admitted. "The girl has talent. She's never a princess in my barn. She's only seven and impresses me most of the time. You're talking a kiddo who's happy to brush, clean hooves and saddle up for herself. She even grabs the plastic fork and scoops poop if one of the horses takes a dump in the arena. Oh, crap. I probably shouldn't have said all that."

"Hey, I enjoyed it. Tell me more."

CHAPTER TWO

Since it was Thanksgiving Day, the cocktail lounge was closed. Well, to everyone alive, that was, but Moises hadn't seen this large crowd of ghosts in months, not since his arrival last summer. Some wore various military uniforms going well back before World War Two. He looked around, spotting women in pioneer dresses, a few in flapper attire from the 1920s, and more in what he considered regular civilian clothes. He saw guys dressed as loggers and miners.

Wearing his usual dark suit, a black fedora shading his face, the mayor circulated among the group. A gray-haired man in a red plaid shirt that jarred with the orange suspenders holding up the cut-off, logging jeans joined the mayor on his rounds, and the two approached Moises.

"This is Newt O'Leary, Moises." Mayor O'Connell nodded a greeting. "He wants a part in the little melodrama you're directing for Christmas, and I promised we'd talk to you about it."

The notion of being the director rather than a participant was a pleasant idea. "I'll need some help, Mayor. I'm new here and I don't know everyone like you do."

"That's his job," Newt announced. "Get on with it, young fella. Tell the folks what we're doing this year. I wanna be the *Ghost of Christmas Present*. That no-good Nick always steals from my hardware store and my kin are tired of dealing with him. Causes holy hell with his family when they hear from the cops. I'll give him the kinda lesson he deserves."

His booming voice attracted attention and the rest of the ghosts drifted closer. Moises glanced around and saw interest rather than disapproval. He hesitantly outlined his idea of reforming Nick MacGillicudy for the holidays. That caused a snort of disgust from one of the women dressed more flamboyantly than the others.

She twirled a red feather boa. "Honey, if that man came to my place back in the day, I'd have shown him the door. I had no room for a lounge lizard who wouldn't pay his shot or tried to take advantage of my gals."

"Faith and bejabbers." This time it was a woman more conservatively attired in a white blouse and long black skirt, beautiful red hair pinned up in a loose bun on her head. "Sure, and you'd have taken pity on the lad if you'd seen how his pa came after him more than oncet and lathered him with a belt in front of half the town."

"We can't all be as kindly minded as you are, Doireann O'Sullivan." Zeke Garvey drawled, standing next to Raven

Driscoll-Barlow, a troop of soldiers behind them. "It's what makes folks recall the lessons you taught them even now. You're right. I remember when Nick won the toy semi-truck at the church Christmas bazaar and Herman took it away and sold it."

Moises saw some of the others nod in agreement. "I haven't been in Baker City that long and I don't know all the people around here like you do. However, I've seen Nick MacGillicudy in action out at Miracle Stable when he went after one of the horses and the new owner fired him. He's not much good as a horseshoer."

"Scuttlebutt is he only does it to try and get folks with large tracts of land to sell them to his dad and his cronies," Newt said. "Like we need more gravel pits around here. We don't. We need our town back. That's what Cat O'Leary-McTavish and folks in the Baker City Business Association are trying to do, and it's why we're helping them."

"Nick should learn nothing he does will be good enough for his pa and quit trying." Florence MacGillicudy, a plump, gray-haired woman in a pioneer dress, spoke up. "When my grand-daughter was a counselor at the high school twenty years ago, Mindy tried telling him that, but the boy never listened."

"It does sound like she made a good choice for someone to follow in her bootsteps out at the stable when she retired and sold Miracle," Mayor O'Connell commented. "And I understand what you folks are saying, but we've all seen that fellow scam-ming drinks from young ladies here at Pop's."

"The apple doesn't fall far from his daddy's tree." This time it was a different, older man who spoke. Moises had often seen him standing behind the bar giving directions to Linda

MacGillicudy or Pop, but they didn't seem to notice the one-time bartender in his light shirt and dark slacks, garters on his sleeves. "I don't remember the number of times Herman claimed to have lost or forgotten his wallet and when I 86'd him back in my day, his pa would raise hell and put props under it."

"Well, let's vote on the proposal Moises Pride has suggested," the mayor said. "When I call for it, all those in favor of using a Baker City version of *A Christmas Carol* to redeem Nick MacGillicudy, say Aye. Those opposed will say, 'Nay.' Anybody undecided?"

"Just another question." A police officer in full regalia waved his hand. "What's to be the final result for young Nick? We can't harm him, or we'll answer to the O'Leary."

"Sure, and he either shapes up or he ships out of our town. No harm, no foul play." Doireann O'Sullivan folded her ghostly arms and nodded sternly. "It fair breaks my heart to see that girl, Kyra O'Neill a-weeping and a-wailing over the wastrel day after day, month after month, year after year. She deserves better than a lay-about."

"We couldn't agree more," Raven told her. "It's why Moises already fixed her up with one of Harry Colter's friends, Sergeant-Major Waller. He reminds me of that tough-guy, Canadian actor on TV, the one who sizzled even if he played a villain. When my husband was on the road, I used to stream that old series where he fought aliens who'd come to destroy Earth and eat all the humans."

"I'd like to see that." The former madam twirled her boa again. "I do enjoy a man who is one, even if I can only look nowadays."

The comment earned laughter from many of the other women, but before Raven could start the TV show, the mayor held up his hand. "We're voting now. All those in favor—"

Thanksgiving or not, forty horses at Miracle Riding Stable still needed to eat. By the time she was out of bed and dressed in a blue staff t-shirt, sweatshirt and faded blue jeans, Kyra heard Trina rustling around in the small kitchen. Time to get up and move. Another day, another dollar. For a moment, Kyra recalled the big paychecks she'd received as a lawyer when she worked for Tex Hawke, then she let the memory go. There were more important things than money, and she wasn't giving up her soul to a politician who didn't have one.

A petite redhead in her mid-twenties, Trina filled a second coffee cup when she saw Kyra. The younger barn manager wore a matching Miracle Stable outfit. "So, how was your date? I was surprised you came home last night. I thought —."

"It was almost a waste of time." Kyra took the mug and sipped the strong, black java, appreciating the jolt of caffeine. "Nick bailed on me again."

"I'm so sorry." Trina frowned, sky-blue eyes narrowing. "Why 'almost' a waste?"

"One of Ann Barrett's and her husband's friends spent nearly two hours trying to pick me up." Kyra laughed. "I'd already eaten because Pop made chicken fettuccine, but I hung out while Waller had a burger. Wasn't any point in coming home, sitting by myself, and sulking over a man who didn't want me. After he ate, Waller convinced me we should play pool."

"Oh, my Gawd! He doesn't know anything about you, does he? Please say you were nice."

"After working with me for the past three years, you should know better than that, Trina." Kyra topped their cups with fresh coffee. "When he suggested a one-night stand with him as a prize, I had no choice."

Trina grinned. "Did you run the table?"

"You know it! While he was scraping his jaw off the floor, I left."

"If anyone ever asks, I'm telling them that you're my hero." Trina dropped two slices of bread in the toaster. "What are your plans for today? Are you coming with me to my grandfather's? Jassy reminded me to invite you again because we both know how you feel about the O'Neill clan. You won't go to one of their houses."

"Never again. I'm staying home. You go have fun and I'll load up on junk food while I watch old holiday movies. And for heaven's sake, tell your sister not to send back any leftovers. I don't need the calories."

"Too bad, too sad. I certainly do."

By noon, Kyra was alone at Miracle Riding Stable. Alone, that was except for the forty horses, the owner's two dogs and two cats. She'd fed the pets, filled their water bowls, and cleaned the litter box. She brought the pups back with her, and the three of them happily watched the big parade on TV. Kyra had told Trina not to rush back. Yes, evening chores would be time-consuming, but it wasn't her first rodeo, as the saying went.

The boss doesn't do church and I don't do holidays. The O'Neill clan put the fun back in dysfunctional, and listening to their arguments would give a saint indigestion. *And that's so not me. I wasn't before I quit being a mouthpiece for Senator Tex Hawke and I'm definitely not one now.* It was something else her relatives regularly bitched about—her leaving a highly paid, highly successful position as an accomplished lawyer in an elite group of political flunkies. Of course, they never understood the stress of that job either.

Working as a barn manager and riding instructor for her rent, her coal-black, Morab gelding's board and a pittance of a salary meant Kyra couldn't spend thousands of dollars on gifts for her parents, sisters, brothers, in-laws and numerous nieces and nephews like she had when she cleaned up Tex Hawke's and Eli Roberts' legal messes. None of the adults understood the need to look at herself in the bathroom mirror in the morning or that trading pieces of her soul was too high a price to pay for financial and professional success.

I owe Mindy MacGillicudy big time. She understood why I walked away five years ago. She offered me a job and a place to live when everyone in my family rejected me. She always quotes that line from Shakespeare about if you're eating with the Devil, you should have a long spoon! Mine wasn't long enough —

Derek moseyed out to the small barn where he found Harry Colter and his stepdaughter taking care of Ann's horse and Devon's pony. It was either helping with farm chores or peeling potatoes for Ann, so he'd exited stage left. He enjoyed the cold, clear morning air, but he spotted snow clouds on the horizon. He closed the door behind him and walked down the center aisle with its eight stalls on the left side. Hay storage, a grain-room and a tack-room were on the right.

"Did you come out here to cowboy up?" In his late thirties, Harry, tall and dark-haired, still looked like a soldier in his civvies, jeans, a flannel shirt, denim jacket and boots. He continued grooming Ann's bay gelding. "Or are you avoiding KP?"

"You know me too well, Colter. Your wife gave me a pass and said she'd put Margo Endicott and her new husband, the Colonel, on it." Derek lingered outside the stall, amused by the carved sign that read, 'Skyrocket'. He'd heard before that Ann rescued the horse after it was injured at a rodeo. "Give me some credit. I was discreet and didn't say issuing orders to officers might be considered inappropriate by some folks."

"Since we don't want to do it, I think you made the right choice, Waller." Harry grinned. "Besides, Ann and Margo will enjoy the chance to gossip. Having her and Sully Murphy both off on maternity leave with their babies at the same time means Ann is busting her butt at the school. She's teaching her students and helping the two replacements with their classes, plus mentoring a third teacher."

"The big kids say Dr. Art is a good teacher," Devon, the little girl, commented. "Mr. Smitty is nice to us, but he's 'most as strict as Aunt Margo. 'Cept, I don't call her that at school. And Ms. Lisa tries real hard, but this is her first job. Sometimes she cries at recess when the kids are mean to her. Mama says she hasta learn not to smile before Christmas next year."

"Baker City School is different from those in bigger districts," Harry explained. "There's only four blended classrooms, Waller. Margo teaches second, third and fourth grades. Lisa Jensen has kindergarten, first grade and a few second-graders. Sully had fifth and sixth graders and Ann's students are in seventh and eighth grade. Devon is in Margo's class because she's an advanced reader and does third-grade math already."

"Mama says I need to be challenged," Devon added. "Or I get in trouble. Last year I got kicked out for fighting at my old school, but somebody needed to kick my cousin's butt and it was my job 'cause he's a bully."

"Except your mama and I agreed you'll leave that to us, Devon." Harry eyed his stepdaughter. "And then I won't rat you out to your karate teacher for going after a third-grader when you were only in first grade."

"Yeah, but Aunt Margo hadn't taken me to karate yet," Devon told him. "I'd do a better job now, but Sensei says good karate-ka's don't pick fights. They just finish 'em."

"And now I'm up to speed on everything," Derek said. "Guess I better not share that Ms. Lisa is one tough officer. She kicks butts and takes no prisoners when she's at the fort, but then she's telling grownups what to do, not little kids."

"Sometimes, there isn't much difference." Harry began brushing Skyrocket's long black tail. "I'll remind Ann to mention it to the LT in their next counseling session."

Derek glanced at the ebony-haired munchkin in the next stall, happily brushing a small black pony who had the distinctive white spots of an Appaloosa. The little girl's hazel eyes held a sparkle of mischief. "What's your horse's name, Devon?"

"Rainy Night. He even has his own song. Mama plays it for me on her phone."

"Amazing." Derek pulled out his cell phone. "Let's see if I can find it too."

A short time later, an older woman came into the barn and strolled toward them. Devon squealed as soon as she saw her, opened the stall door, and raced to greet her. "Ms. Mindy! Ms. Mindy! Mama said you might come. Where's Ms. Kyra?"

"Not with me." The elderly white-haired woman hadn't dressed up for the occasion. She wore jeans, a plaid, western shirt with pearl snaps, and lace-up riding boots. She nodded and held out a hand to Derek. "I'm Mindy MacGillicudy. Devon takes lessons at Miracle Stable. I used to own it."

"And Ms. Kyra is my teacher now, 'cept when I did horse camp last summer." Devon informed him. "Then I had lots of teachers. Where are they?"

"Let's see. Ms. Debbie took her girls and went to visit her boys at college in Eastern Washington. Ms. Trina is probably with her older sister and grandpa."

"And Jason and Carol are big kids, so they're at home too." Worry swept across Devon's face. "That means Ms. Kyra is all by herself. That's not fair."

"What's not?" Derek asked.

"She has to take care of all the horses by herself." Devon turned toward Harry. "She's gotta muck and water and feed lots and lots of them. Can't we go help her? She says I'm her best pooper-scooper. And it will be forever till dinner. If we help, she can come here too. Mama won't mind."

"Before you say that, shouldn't you ask her?" Derek winked at the other adults. "And it sounds like a good idea to me. I don't know anything about cleaning stalls, but maybe the best pooper-scooper could teach me. What do you think, Devon?"

"I don't know. You're kinda old. Not as old as Ms. Mindy." Devon eyed him critically. "I only teach the other kids who skip what Ms. Debbie calls the 'maverick' poops. You haveta put all the clumps in the muck tub and you can't put fresh shavings over 'em and try to hide 'em. If you do, then the horses lie on them and get all dirty and smelly."

Mindy looked amused by the lecture on stall cleaning. "Does Ms. Debbie actually say clumps? I'd think after being a soldier she'd have other words."

"Oh, she does, but Ms. Kyra told her we can't say, 'turds' because it upsets the mommies and daddies and grandpas and grandmas. So, no more potty mouths." Devon snagged Derek's hand. "Come on, Sarge-Maje. Let's go tell Mama 'bout Ms. Kyra. Then, we'll go to Miracle. I know the way."

"I bet you do." Derek allowed himself to be towed toward the door. He hadn't expected the opportunity to see Kyra O'Neill so soon, but he'd take advantage of it. He glanced over his shoulder at Harry and Mindy. "Come along, you two. It sounds like there will be plenty of horsy poo to share. When we get back, I'll help out here."

"Compared to forty of the critters, two are nothing," Mindy informed him. "I could muck, water and feed Sky and Rainy Night in twenty minutes even if I am older than dirt."

"Yes, but you won't have the chance." Harry sauntered beside her. "My grandma will be here soon, and she'd never let me hear the end of it if I let a guest do my horse chores. Plus, I'm pretty sure Ann would kick my backside if I was that rude to people she'd invited here."

CHAPTER THREE

The ghosts in the cocktail lounge continued discussing who would have principal roles in the upcoming drama, but everyone agreed that Moises should play Marley and let Nick MacGillicudy know what was in store for him.

"Tis only fair," Doireann O'Sullivan said. "Sure, and we don't want him to miss the lesson we'll be a-teaching him."

"How will he see me?" Moises asked. "Most folks don't. It's why they depend on Cat O'Leary-McTavish and her husband to tell them what we want."

"He has enough O'Leary blood in him to make this work, young feller, and his momma is one of my kin." Newt O'Leary looked around the tavern. "The MacGillicudys are like the rest of the families here. We're all related if you go back far enough."

"And even if you don't." Mayor O'Connell glanced toward the doorway as Raven Driscoll-Barlow entered the lounge again. "What did you learn?"

"Nick just showed up for the holiday dinner. When his cousin, Dray, pointed out the donation can to him, Nick refused to pay anything for the meal." Raven wrinkled her ghostly nose in disgust. "Does he think Pop and his daughter have won the lottery? That they can afford to feed the town for free?"

"They'd have to buy tickets first," Florence told her. "And my brother's boy isn't one to waste his money." She turned to Moises. "Go wait in his truck so you'll be there when he leaves. Raven is barely waiting to turn on that silly TV show of hers so she can show us what that hero you've chosen for Kyra O'Neill looks like."

Moises followed orders. He knew better than to ignore what a granny told him and drifted out to the parking lot. Another good thing about being a ghost was he didn't have to break into the rig. He floated through the door and sat in the passenger seat. Time to *hurry up and wait* for the civilian to join him. Once he'd been warned, Zeke Garvey would haunt him tonight and share memories of previous holidays. *Let the fun begin!*

As always, the traditional dinner at Pop's Café in Baker City was much better than any of the ones he'd endure at his relatives' homes, Nick MacGillicudy thought. Nobody bitched if he avoided the stuffing and loaded up on mashed potatoes and gravy. Plus, Pop MacGillicudy usually served three different kinds of meat, turkey, ham, and prime rib. Granted, his father's cousin put out a donation can, but Nick figured if he planned to pay for a meal, he'd go to a restaurant in Lake Maynard, not a place owned by a MacGillicudy.

Although he'd enjoyed the holiday buffet from the appetizers to that final piece of his favorite pecan pie topped with vanilla ice-cream, he couldn't take home any leftovers. He'd miss having a turkey sandwich layered with cranberry sauce tonight. That was one disadvantage of avoiding his family. Still, he didn't have to listen to his father talking about his plans and schemes to bulldoze Baker City and turn the town into a giant gravel pit. A little of that went a long way, and the ensuing arguments among family members was enough to spoil any and every holiday.

Nick unlocked the driver's door of his Ford 250 and slid behind the wheel of the pickup. He started the engine, shifted into gear. Now, he'd head for Lake Maynard and go drinking. It was too early to go home.

"Whoa. Aren't you putting on your seat belt?" a man asked. "It's against the law to drive without one."

Nick slammed on the brakes and stared at the stranger in the passenger seat. "What the hell? How did you get in my truck? Now, get out!"

Suddenly, he realized he could see through the shadowy figure of a young, African-American with close-cropped black hair. The guy wore camouflage fatigues, combat boots and had a beret stuffed in one pants' pocket. Slowly, Nick put the truck back in park. "Who the hell are you?"

"Call me, Marley." The soldier smiled, a quick gleam of white teeth in the dark afternoon. "I came to warn you, Nicholas Herman MacGillicudy to change your ways."

"What?" Nick stared at the man but didn't see any wires or cameras around. "Are you serious? I don't believe this. Did my sister, Dominique pay you to put on the act?"

"She didn't need to. You're from Baker City and you have O'Leary heritage. Time to grow up and act like a man. You're about to have three visitors."

"Are you one of them?" Nick snickered. "I think you've been watching too many Hallmark movies. Christmas is for suckers, and I'm not into chick flicks."

"Neither am I." Marley shifted in the seat. Suddenly a blood-drenched image of him appeared. A shattered bone stuck out below his knee. Blood poured from a giant wound through his ribs. Surprisingly, he laughed and mocked. "Do you hear me now, Mac?"

Shocked, Nick gaped at him and then heard a distant gunshot. More than half of Marley's head disappeared, replaced with a bloody mass. "Oh, my God! What the hell? What is that?"

"How I died." The gruesome injuries faded, and Marley returned to a ghostly normal. "Like I said, you have a chance to redeem yourself. If I were you, I'd take it."

Marley faded away and Nick gazed at the empty seat. No stranger. No blood on the side window or windshield from when he'd heard the gunshot and seen its bloody aftermath. Nothing, not even the coppery odor of blood or the smell of rotting flesh.

He shuddered, realized the engine was racing, and took his foot off the accelerator. He reached over his shoulder, pulled on his seatbelt. For a moment, Nick contemplated the trip to Lake Maynard and then he changed his mind. He'd go home.

Nobody would be in or around his trailer. He'd be safe there. He hoped.

After lunch, Kyra headed for the first barn to collect grain buckets, clean stalls, and water. It'd take at least two hours to do all three barns, but whatever she did would make evening chores easier. All she'd have to do at the end of the day was scoop the last few piles of horsy poo and then feed supper hay.

She was in the middle of cleaning the third stall when what Debbie called the doggie alarms went off. Shasta, the almost grown, shaggy tri-colored collie mix and Bonzer, the four-month-old, gray, and black cattle puppy bolted toward the end of the barn, barking madly at a group of people.

Kyra watched them approach, recognizing Mindy MacGillicudy, the previous owner of the business. The army sergeant who'd tried so hard to pick her up the previous night, Derek Waller, Harry Colter, and little Devon Sweeney-Barrett accompanied the elderly woman. The girl began petting and praising the dogs.

"What's going on?" Kyra focused on the adults. "I know Trina closed and padlocked the highway gates. She's super responsible that way. Why are you here?"

"I still have a key, Ms. Snarky. Debbie said I could visit whenever I wanted, so there's no point calling the cops." Mindy grinned at her. "We came to share the work with you, and then you'll be able to join us for dinner."

"I've got this." Kyra leaned on the fork for a moment while

the golden palomino pony stuck his head over the stall door, in a search for carrots. "I didn't ask for any help."

"We've been volunteered." Derek gestured toward Devon. "She promised to teach me how to find maverick horse stuff when I muck stalls and I'm willing to learn."

"I don't believe this." Kyra tried to remind herself that she was crazy about Nick MacGillicudy, but why wasn't it working? Maybe it was because he'd never offered to help her with anything at Miracle Stable in the past five years. They just had casual hookups and only if she tracked him down to jump his bones. Sex happened on an intermittent basis and sometimes it wasn't that good. *So, why am I pretending what we have is real?*

Kyra scanned Derek again. Stonewashed jeans hugged long legs and a black, military sweater clung to broad shoulders, muscular arms, and a wide chest. She met his amused, dark gaze and smiled at him. Even in what they undoubtedly referred to as civvies, he and Harry looked lethal, and she wasn't sure they'd cheerfully accept a refusal.

Mindy wouldn't. They'd shared enough holidays over the last five years to accept each other's baggage.

And Kyra wasn't about to hurt Devon's feelings. "Okay, Devon. Stop playing with the dogs and take these fellows to find poop forks. Mindy, will you fill the water tubs? I don't know about dinner—"

"Mama said, 'more the merrier' and we gotta bring you back or Harry has to do all the dishes and no whining 'cause she wouldn't let him put in a big dishwasher and wreck her old-fashioned, real kitchen counters."

"Colonel Williams and I will be stuck helping him with KP,"

Derek added. "You have to save us from that, or we'll be on the battalion commander's sh—" He stopped when he saw the censorious look from Harry. "Let's make that a hit list."

"What's that mean?" Devon asked.

"We'll have lots of stinky jobs to do at the base, Princess Devon, and neither of us wants to be stuck with them," Harry told her. "Put on your equestrian helmet and show us what we have to do."

"You got it." With the tri-colored collie-mix and the heeler puppy following along, Devon led the way to the hay-room where supplies were stored.

"Talk to me." Kyra stared at Mindy. "I haven't gone anywhere for Thanksgiving in years. How am I supposed to show up at Ann Barrett's when I don't have anything to share?"

"I took two big pumpkin pies and they're already waiting at Ann's and Harry's." Mindy patted Kyra's hand. "We're covered, honey. And both of us need to stop letting people like most of the MacGillicudys and O'Neills control so much of our minds, thoughts, feelings, hearts, and emotions. Time for us to grow up."

"Is that some of your headshrinker talk?"

"Yes, but it's much easier to pass the advice onto the folks in my therapy groups than it is to take it myself." Mindy sighed. "Help me out here, Kyra."

"All right, but it still feels a little scary."

"You're preaching to the proverbial choir, girlfriend."

Derek never thought of impressing a woman by shoveling horse manure, but a guy did what he had to do. It surprised him that the barn really didn't smell like manure or urine. Instead, he caught the scent of hay, shavings, and grain. Each horse had its own water tub and those varied in color from barn to barn. Mindy didn't have to dump or scrub more than one or two in each stable. She told him the rest were cleaned on a regular basis. The pups patrolled the hallways and plopped down for occasional naps, a credit to their owner's training. Kyra said the boss didn't allow them to enter the stalls and upset the horses.

To be honest, the work wasn't that big of a deal. He'd completed harder tasks in the army. Each horse only had two or three piles of crap in its stall along with some wet shavings. All of it ended up in large plastic containers at the back of the individual stalls. Devon explained Señor Gonzales, the new ranch-hand dumped those tubs three times a week. Before he'd started working at Miracle Riding Stable, Kyra and Jason, one of the assistant instructors, did it.

"You're a strong woman." Derek glanced at Kyra who cleaned one of the adjacent stalls. "I bet those tubs get heavy."

"It wasn't bad because we alternated barns and did one of them each day, so it meant the tubs got dumped twice a week. Jason loves driving the garden tractor and barely lets me have a turn." Kyra spread fresh pine shavings over the bedding. The red horse snorted, then took another dump on top of them. "Thanks a lot, Copper. Everyone loves a smartie."

"That's one word for it." Derek admired the fact that she didn't make a big deal of picking up the last pile before leaving the stall. It took him longer to clean than it did her or the other people, but he improved as he went along. When they finished mucking, he helped feed the livestock their lunch hay. Afterwards, Kyra took the two dogs back to the large three-story house. Mindy said she'd wait for her friend and ride back with Kyra to Harry's place.

"We'll wait for you too," Derek said. "We can follow you there."

"Let's turn that around," Kyra told him. "I haven't been to the Colter place before. I'll get changed and be with you in a few minutes."

"Sounds good." Harry gestured toward his truck. "Let's mosey, folks." When they stood near the pickup and Devon had climbed into the back seat, he glanced at Derek. "Haven't seen you pursue a woman in a while. What's different this time?"

"She is." Derek reached for the pack of cigarettes he used to carry in his shirt pocket, then recalled he'd stopped smoking on doctor's orders after his last physical. He fished out a stick of spearmint gum instead. "She's sharp and doesn't take crap. Beat me at pool last night."

"Don't *Bravo Sierra* me. I've seen you hustle too many folks to augment your very good salary." Harry chuckled. "Why did you let her win?"

"It was a distraction, Colter. I figured she'd lose the next game, but she left while I racked the balls."

"You're right. She's good," Harry said. "And you definitely deserve her."

Derek whistled softly as the women came toward them. Kyra had changed into a gold embroidered western shirt under a denim jacket, clean dress jeans and boots similar to what Mindy wore. Kyra O'Neill hadn't tried to upstage her mentor and it showed real class. She wore a knitted, red stocking hat, but most of her ash-blonde hair swung free from its braid. Makeup highlighted the gray eyes and long lashes. She hadn't overdone the cosmetics. So damned elegant. No wonder she'd impressed him last night and then again today. "Let's go to dinner."

CHAPTER FOUR

When they reached the Colter property, there were at least a half-dozen vehicles parked in front of the large, two-story log house. With Derek Waller beside her, Kyra walked next to Mindy toward the wrap-around porch, following Harry and Devon. They entered through the mud-room and went into the kitchen. Harry crossed the room and hugged his grandmother, Janine O'Connell, who'd just arrived. Devon immediately made the rounds, hugging and being hugged by the visitors.

Several people were already in the room, ranging from Margo Endicott, the red-haired woman cuddling a sleeping baby, her husband, Jared Williams, a tall man built like a truck driver to Frank and Ginger Madison, Ann's parents, owners of the fancy Morgan breeding stable on the other side of town. Jack, Ann's younger brother, was there too, and Kyra counted her blessings when she saw him holding a soda. He was a known party animal and one of Nick's close associates. They often took up space at the bar in the cocktail lounge in Pop's Café on Friday and Saturday nights.

Kyra paused in the doorway allowing everyone else the opportunity to interact, grateful Baker City was a small town, and she already knew most of the other guests. It was her first visit, and she took a moment to admire the vintage cedar cupboards, matching butcher-block countertops, the hardwood floor, farmhouse sink, the antique enameled woodstove, appreciating the fact there wasn't any 'granite' or 'laminate' in sight. She spotted old-style white appliances, a refrigerator, upright freezer, and electric range, but she didn't see a dishwasher anywhere.

She suppressed a smile, looking over her shoulder at Derek. "You were serious about the dishes, weren't you?"

"I never joke about KP, honey." He winked at her before turning to Ann Barrett who sliced tomatoes at the counter. "We're back from the barns, so how can we help?"

"First, wash your hands." Ann gestured in the direction of the hallway. "Devon, show your teacher where the bathroom is and after that, I need you to check on your dog. See if Shadow needs to go outside."

"Okay. Come on, Miss Kyra."

When she returned to the kitchen, Kyra found herself helping Ginger Madison with the fruit salad. The older woman had opted for ironed jeans, a crisp western blouse and laced-up cowgirl boots. Her blonde hair came from the bottle now and didn't dare show a hint of gray. She pasted on a professionally friendly smile. It didn't touch her hazel eyes as she asked about fall programs at Miracle Riding Stable.

"Frank was impressed the new owner already had a horse-show." Ginger continued to cut Fuji apples into quarters. "She only moved here in August. He said it took him three years to host a show at Majestyk Morgans."

"Oh, but Debbie had Kyra and Trina to help." Mindy spread a fancy tablecloth on the long wooden table in the middle of the room. "The stable has always catered to local, beginning riders, not the high-end clientele you and Frank handle. It was my specialty, and I'm glad Debbie is providing more programs for them."

"They come in all sizes, and everyone seems happy with what we're doing now." Kyra peeled another banana and sliced it. "After almost twenty years in the Army, Debbie knows how to delegate. She organized different parents to do different things like getting Heather McElroy have Hawke Construction help Trina with the trail course."

That earned a brilliant smile from Ginger. "Devon won second place on Rainy Night in the obstacle course. Frank was thrilled when she asked him to help her make a trophy wall in her room."

Kyra slowly realized the older woman wasn't standoffish, but rather painfully shy. Okay, after teaching a variety of children, tweens, and teens for five years plus her experience as a lawyer, she knew how to keep the dialogue flowing and make another person feel comfortable. During the rest of the conversation, Kyra didn't change the subject. She asked open-ended questions and encouraged Ginger to talk all about her beloved, albeit somewhat spoiled, granddaughter.

While Janine O'Connell and Kyra set the table, they

discussed the day-care Janine had operated in Baker City for years. Kyra promised to drop off more brochures for her popular, little kid classes for three-and four-year-olds. "The munchkins are always excited about brushing and saddling their ponies prior to riding them. I insist on parents or grandparents being ready and willing to help the children with everything from feeding carrots to cleaning hooves to eventually assisting the kiddoes with independent riding."

"It's a really popular activity," Janine said. "I have so many clients who want to do it with their youngsters. The problem is you only offer the class on Fridays and there's such a long waiting list. Any chance you could do it on Wednesday and Thursday mornings, too?"

"I'll ask Debbie next week when she returns from eastern Washington." Kyra worked her way around the table, placing napkins beside the mismatched, stoneware plates. The sight amused her, especially when she recalled her mother's insistence on pulling out perfect china for holidays. Woe betide the person who accidentally broke a saucer or teacup.

Kyra paused to glance around the room again. Small talk ebbed and flowed as everyone helped put together the traditional meal. It was totally different from the days when she went to dinner with the O'Neill clan. Then, the men and boys tended to congregate in living-rooms to watch football while the women and girls bustled around the kitchen and dining room cooking and chatting.

Devon was engaged in assisting her uncle. The two of them happily put olives, pickles, and jams in small dishes, which the little girl carried to the table. Meantime, her mother stirred gravy at the stove while Harry carved the turkey at one of the counters. Derek was in charge of filling glasses with sparkling cider.

Slowly, Kyra realized she was happy. This was much better than eating a microwave dinner in her carriage-style apartment in the loft of the barn adjacent to the indoor arena at Miracle Riding Stable. She took the silverware from Mindy. "Thank you for inviting me today."

"You're welcome, but it was Devon's idea. She's a treasure. I'm glad she thought of it."

"Me too," Kyra said.

Derek sat next to Kyra during dinner. He hadn't been at a holiday family meal in years but enjoyed this one more than he'd hoped. Topics of conversation ranged from Devon's and Ann's school days to work at Fort Bronson to horse activities at the two very different barns to day-time TV shows, Margo Endicott's contribution. Being home with her new son meant her days varied widely from teaching second, third and fourth grade. Now, she claimed she often had the opportunity to languish on the sofa or in a rocking chair or recliner during the afternoon while her son slept.

Mindy brought up the subject of Christmas. "Kyra, did you mention to Debbie what we've always done at Miracle before she left for Pullman?"

A flush brightened Kyra's cheeks and she shook her head.

"My bad. We were so busy talking about the riding schedule for the weekend it completely slipped my mind."

"What do you do there?" Derek asked. "It must include horse care."

"Everything does, but my students also decorate their stall doors. Trina's clubs and the boarders do theirs too. We have a big Christmas party on horseback and gift exchange on the second Saturday in December when we give prizes for the different doors." Kyra glanced at Frank Madison. "What do you do over at your place?"

"Lots of decorations around our viewing area and in the staff lounge, but we don't put up anything in the barns because I don't want to take down decorations after New Year's Day," Frank said. "We have a party for the grooms, exercise riders and trainers. Ginger always shops for those presents. All I have to do is write the bonus checks. We order gift baskets for our clients and thankfully those are delivered for us. Otherwise, I'd spend weeks driving all over the U.S. to take them to my customers."

"You're lucky to have Mother to rescue you, Dad." Ann flicked a sideways glance at her husband. "Don't think I'm gonna save you from the stores, Colter. If I have to go, you do too."

"I love shopping," Ginger announced. "Give me your list and the money and I'll snag Devon after school a few days and we'll visit all the malls."

Devon nodded enthusiastically. "Yeah, then I get to see Santa lots and lots of times."

"Let me know when we're going," Janine said. "It can't be this weekend because I'm opening the day care early for all my regular clients who want to hit the sales sans kiddoes, but they're picked up by six at night and I can meet you in Lake Maynard."

"Works for us," Ginger decided. "Right, Devon?"

"Right!" Devon immediately agreed.

"And it works for me too, Mother. I'm definitely taking you up on it." Ann picked up her glass and sipped cider. "What about you, Waller? Are you good with stores or do they bother you like they still do me? I nearly went nuts at the grocery the other day. The crowds—"

"It gets easier with time, Barrett." Derek eyed her and then turned his attention to Margo. "What about you, Captain? Do you go to the grocery now?"

"Not me." Margo looked at the baby sleeping in the portable bassinet next to her chair. "I text Jared and he picks up whatever we need. I'm like Ann. After that last stint in the *sandbox*, I'm not ready to deal with people yet, especially those who leave their manners at home. I nearly smacked one know-it-all guy who tried to tell me what to do with my crying baby two weeks ago when I popped into the mercantile to pick up our mail."

"Took a while for me to adjust after one of my bad tours back in the day." Jared Williams covered Margo's hand with his. "Like Waller says, it gets better. Cut yourselves some slack."

"And call or text me," Kyra added. "I'm like Ginger. I love shopping especially when I'm spending somebody else's money. I've known Maxine Garvey, the postmaster in Baker City, forever so if you need someone to get your mail, I'll do it when I collect mine."

"And you'd better contact Debbie and see what the budget is

for tomorrow," Mindy said. "I'll pick you up at four-thirty and we'll hit the Black Friday bargain sales."

"What about the horses?" Derek focused on the woman beside him. "Do you go to the barn at oh-dark-thirty before the shopping excursion? Do you want help? After today's training, I'm not an expert, but I can learn."

"Not needful." Kyra smiled, amusement lighting her gray eyes. "Since I do most of the chores on Thanksgiving, Trina picks them up on Black Friday. We have two high school students who will be in to help her. I just need to get my new boss on board. I'll do that when she checks in this evening."

"And then you can text me," Derek said. "You've got to save me from one of Colter's projects. I don't know what it will be, but I'm pretty sure it will—" He paused and hastily cleaned up his proverbial potty mouth. Ever since his buddy married a woman with a little girl, Harry didn't allow cussing around the kid, and it'd taken an effort to remember the rules today. "I'd much rather go shopping with two gorgeous gals because I know whatever Colter has in mind will stink."

"No, it won't, Waller, but go ahead and evade hauling firewood while you can. There will be plenty to stack in the woodshed when you return."

"I'll stop by for a few hours and give you a hand, Colter," Jared said. "Margo won't want me around in the afternoon when she and Garrett are napping. Afterwards, I'll go into town to the bakery and get cheesecake."

That earned a smile from Margo. "You do know what makes me happy."

More laughter from the people around the table, especially

when Ann announced she'd ordered a selection of various kinds of Twila's specialties. "Plus, we have my favorite pumpkin pie from Mindy. I love the way she tops it with pecan streusel."

After dinner and the dishes, almost everyone bundled up and headed outdoors to tramp around the property on a hunt for the perfect Christmas trees. Margo agreed to stay behind and entertain Ann's parents and Harry's grandmother. Ginger gave Ann a roll of bright red survey tape so she could tag the ever-greens. It was dry and cold. The sun had burned away most of the clouds and it'd warmed up to almost 40 degrees. Devon and her nearly grown collie mix, Shadow ran races around the adults.

Derek glanced at Harry. "Where's your axe or chainsaw? How are you going to cut down trees without one or the other?"

"I already got the word from the boss." Harry snagged Ann's hand. "No pine tree murders this season. Saturday, I'll come out and dig up the ones she wants for us, Margo, her folks, and Grandma. After Christmas, I'm planting them in everybody's yards."

"And I'll be helping this weekend and then after the holi-day," Jared said.

"Brilliant." Kyra flashed a smile. "I'm going to suggest that to the new boss at Miracle."

"How many does she want?" Harry asked.

"Don't worry. We have tons of cedars in the woodlot at the stable. She'll probably have her husband and Pedro do the honors." Kyra adjusted the red knit hat over her blonde hair. "We always put up one in the office, a second in the lunch-room for the kids, a third in my apartment—"

"And a taller one in the living-room at my old house," Mindy finished. "Tell Debbie she has to bring one over to my cabin at the dude ranch. I'll put Heather and Durango in charge of the one at the vet center."

"Sounds like everybody has holiday plans." Derek fished out his pack of gum and handed it around, sharing pieces with the others. "I know what I'll be doing on Saturday."

"What's that?" Kyra asked. "Resting up after our big shopping trip tomorrow?"

"Nope. I'll be digging up trees with Colter and Williams. Can't let them have all the fun."

CHAPTER FIVE

Thanksgiving night when he entered the cocktail lounge, Moises found Zeke Garvey sitting alone at a table. Because the place closed early on the holiday, none of the living folks in Baker City were here. He drifted across the room to join the other Army Ranger. "Are you ready to visit Nick MacGillicudy tonight?"

"I'm looking forward to it." Zeke glanced around the room at the rest of the ghosts. Several of the women clustered close to the television, watching the classic, 1980's science-fiction series Raven had chosen before she left the lounge. "Appreciate you coming up with this, Pride. Holidays are a tough time of year."

"Really? Why?" Moises eased into the opposite chair, deciding he should step up and listen to the man's troubles. "Usually, Raven Barlow hangs out with you. Where is she?"

"Went to visit her namesake, baby Raven Murphy and her

twin sis, Reveille, the daughters of her BFF, Sully and her husband, Tate Murphy. They'll be home from his parents' place by now. Told our Raven, I'd meet her back here after I checked in on my family."

Moises blinked. It was the first time he'd heard the former Army Ranger had people here in Baker City. He'd just figured the rest of the ghosts were happy to find somewhere like Baker City where they could be comfortable and accepted, plus they had their own medium, Cat O'Leary-McTavish to run interference with the living.

"I didn't know you had anyone who lived in Baker City, but then again, I don't know everyone around here," Moises said. "Who are they?"

"The Garveys. I miss being with all of them at Thanksgiving, especially my wife, Twila. She followed me from Army base to Army base for so long and waited patiently with our sons every time I shipped out on another combat tour."

"How many boys do you have, Garvey?"

"Five of them. My mother says they're just like me and my brothers, rough, tough, and wild, but I always insisted they respect their mother. Followed the same rules my dad set for me and my bros not to sass Momma."

"Five sons." Moises whistled softly. "Wow, that's a houseful."

"Twila always wanted a little girl. She thought she might be pregnant when I shipped out the last time. Surprise, surprise. She was and we finally had our baby daughter. Wish I was around to remind the boys to look after her."

"You are here," Moises pointed out. "Have you talked to the O'Leary and asked her to give messages to your wife and kids?"

"I hadn't thought of it." Zeke frowned, obviously considering the idea. "That might work. I know Raven tells the O'Leary what she wants Sully to hear."

For the next hour, Moises listened to more of Zeke's stories about his wife. He met Twila Desmond in high school, and they'd been together ever since. She followed him all over the continental U.S., to Alaska and Europe when he made a career out of the military. She always found a job where he was stationed, usually in a restaurant because she trained as a pastry chef. They planned to move back home to Baker City when he retired from the Army. She'd brought the kids and come home to be close to his family after he died and opened a bakery to support herself and their children. Zeke visited the place almost every day.

When he finished describing his wife and kids, Zeke detailed his plans for haunting Nick MacGillicudy. Moises added a few ideas and then sent the older Army Ranger to complete his assignment. Spotting Newt O'Leary and Mayor O'Connell in the corner booth, Moises floated across the room and joined them. Now, he'd listen to the next ghost so they could plan tomorrow night's adventure.

Be afraid, Nick, be very afraid!

Kyra found Jacinth Sweeney helping her younger sister, Trina, finish the feeding at Miracle Riding Stable that afternoon. Kyra eyed the junior riding instructor. "What's going on? I thought Jassy was large and in charge of the holiday dinner at the family ranch. Isn't she the resident caretaker for your grandpa and the doormat for the rest of the Sweeneys?"

"You know she hates it when you say stuff like that especially since it's close to the truth. Things got a bit sticky this afternoon, and she needs somewhere to stay." Trina gestured for Kyra to follow her out of earshot. "I told her it'd be okay if she bunked with us for the weekend until she straightened out her affairs."

"What kind of sticky?" Kyra leaned against the tackroom door. "Did she have a fight with her boyfriend, Laredo?"

"Oh no. He's a sweetie and he wasn't there. He was at his older brother's place. Grandpa Sweeney announced he's changing his will and the old Sweeney homestead is going to his new foreman unless one of the guys steps up and takes over the spread. It can be an uncle, my dad, or even the distant cousins. The key thing is that it must be a man whose offspring will bear the Sweeney name."

"Are you serious? What's wrong with him? Is he off his meds?" Kyra stared past Trina to the far end of the barn at the other redhead. "Everybody in town knows Jassy does everything for him plus working her butt off on the place and holding as many part-time jobs as she can to support it."

"Yeah, well Grandpa is old-school, and he says women should only have careers until they marry. Jassy will be thirty next year and doesn't have a husband in sight. If or when Jacinth marries Laredo and starts popping out kids, they'll be Hawkes, not Sweeneys, because he won't change his last name. And Grandpa thinks Laredo is a wuss because other than that thing about his name, he lets Jassy boss him around. So, if one of the male Sweeneys doesn't step up, then Grandpa says it will go to a Hawke with balls."

"Are you serious?" Kyra repeated. "Jassy and Laredo Hawke have dated forever. If he had half a brain, he'd have proposed years ago. He can't do better. Nobody else would have stood beside him when he was drinking and drugging or insist, he call his sponsor when he's losing it."

"He's clean and —"

"I know." Kyra held up her hand to stop the words. "I know. You're going to beat me up with the fact that he's been clean and sober for five years. Don't forget I saw him in action when he lived at home. His parents were constantly trying to get him to straighten up and nothing they did worked."

"I forgot you were there when he was a kid."

"Him and his sisters. They ran wild in Washington D.C. when Congress was in session, and I was constantly sent to rectify the legal conundrums when they were arrested." Kyra shook her head. "Never mind. The past is the past. I'm the first to admit Jassy irritates me with her saintly attitude, willingness to turn the other cheek and the way she always helps her neighbors without rubbing their noses in it. Hopefully, staying with us will put some starch in her girdle as one of my professors used to say, and she'll tell your misogynistic grandfather to kiss her butt when he wants her back."

Trina grinned appreciatively. "From your mouth to Santa's list of good kids. Anything else, Ms. Snarky?"

"Yeah, when she wants an employment contract from your grandpa before she goes home to be a doormat, let me know. I'll write it up for her."

"I wish." Trina heaved a sigh. "You know she won't let you. She always puts everybody else first and they always crap on her. My parents and older sisters are calling and texting me to send her back home. Then, the aunts and uncles started in on me. They want her to suck up to Grandpa because they don't want to look after him. I turned off my phone and figured you'd call me on the landline if the world stopped turning."

"Good for you." Kyra frowned thoughtfully. "Why aren't they calling her direct?"

"Because she threw her cell phone in Grandpa's face and told him to call someone who cares and it's not her. On our way here, I texted Laredo and he said we could drop her dog, Rounder at his place. No worries, 'cause Laredo was the one who gave him to her."

"That was decent of him," Kyra said.

"Yeah, well he also said he'd tell his cousin, Bendigo to feed her horses when he got back to the Sweeney place."

"What does he have to do with anything?"

"Grandpa hired him to be the new foreman."

"That makes no sense, Trina. His family owns huge spreads in Texas. If he wanted to play cowboy, he could do it there for a lot more money than what the Sweeneys can pay."

"You're telling me. He claims he only accepted the offer as a temporary measure while he recuperated since he was injured on his last trip to South America. Grandpa said Bendigo would stay if he had a *real* job here and now Jassy can do what a woman should."

"How did Bendigo even wind up there in the first place?"

"Jassy found him passed out at Pop's last month. She took Bendigo home with her to recover before he went back to Nighthawke Security at the dude ranch so he wouldn't be embarrassed in front of the other mercenaries."

"Okay, so then Jassy needs to tell your grandpa she's done and where he can go," Kyra said sweetly. "Oh, and all the young ones too! And I'm including your dad and his brothers on that list."

Trina laughed and nodded in agreement. "Well, let's try to convince Jassy that taking time for herself is the right thing to do."

"Definitely." While they helped feed the rest of the horses, Kyra remembered the past. When she graduated from law school, she'd turned down several offers from prestigious firms to take a job with Senator Tex Hawke and his team. She intended to save the country and the world, not look after his spoiled brats and condescending, pompous wife. *I'm not Mary Poppins. I left before the wind changed direction.*

At 0330 hours, Derek wasn't the first one to hit the kitchen for coffee. To his amazement, he found Ann Barrett sitting at the table, a cup in front of her. She wore a blue fleece bathrobe, and he glimpsed a touch of lace in the opening at her neck. He didn't look any lower. He wasn't an officer, but he was a gentleman. Shoulder-length auburn hair foamed around her face. It wasn't pinned up in the bun she wore for military duty.

She forked up more of Mindy MacGillicudy's delicious pumpkin pie. "I'm calling this breakfast or a late-night snack. Take your pick."

"What's happening, Barrett?" Derek filled a mug with strong, black coffee and after a moment, topped her cup. "Did you and Colter have a spat? He can be a —"

"He's perfectly fine. Sound asleep and I had another nightmare." Ann narrowed her green eyes. "If you tell me that time heals all issues, I'll throw this coffee at you."

Derek put the cup on the table and went in search of a saucer and fork so he could help himself to the pie in the serving dish. "Want to share what the dreams are about?"

"Not really." Ann took another bite. "I'd rather think about how on earth Mindy creates the pecan streusel topping for this. I wonder if she'd give me the recipe. I asked her yesterday and she wasn't receptive. She said it was a family secret."

"Then there's only one thing to do." Derek sat opposite her and reached for the server, cutting himself a slab of pumpkin pie. "Want to hear it?"

"Sure. Go for it, Waller. What's your suggestion?"

"Ask Linda MacGillicudy and if she turns you down, talk to the woman that Colter calls, the O'Leary. According to him, she knows where all the bodies are buried."

Ann laughed. "And if she can get the recipe from one of them, I'm covered with Mindy. I'll tell her where Cat got it."

"Works for me." Derek waited while they ate pie and drank coffee. He tried probing about the nightmare again, but Ann refused to share. In a way, he didn't blame her. Three of the soldiers from her unit died during their last combat tour in Afghanistan, plus a junior officer who'd been visiting from a headquarters company.

She'd been home for eight months, but Harry said Ann couldn't make herself visit their graves at the Fort Bronson military cemetery. However, she interacted with Sully Barlow-Murphy, who'd survived that ambush even before the other teacher joined the staff at the Baker City school.

Derek drank more coffee. "So, did Colter share what we learned when we visited the new base in Liberty Valley? The battalion will move there after the holidays."

"He showed me pictures on his phone and said something about his new office being larger than the one Jared Williams has in our current building." Ann paused for thought. "What about you, Derek? What happens to your job when the reserve units move away from Fort Bronson, and it's turned into a park?"

"This is just between us. You, me, and Colter. I haven't turned in my resignation yet, but I did tell Williams that thirty years in this man's army is enough. Colter will take over my job and manage the day-to-day business for all the Army Reserve units at Fort Darby. It means a promotion and pay increase."

"And more responsibility." Ann propped her chin on her fist. "He'll need a secretary to handle the paperwork for him and answer phones. Who do you have in mind for that?"

"Still taking applications and we'll begin interviewing in two weeks." Derek winked at her. "We'll give preference to men, not women who might chase your man."

Ann laughed. "Oh, I'm not worried about competition,

Waller. Just find the best person for the job to make it easy on Harry. I do enough whining about my job right now. He doesn't get to complain very often."

"I'll keep that in mind."

"And what are you going to do?" Ann asked. "I can't see you sleeping behind a stump."

"Oh, I'm going to open a car repair place here in Baker City. People can buy parts at the hardware store from Aiden O'Leary, but if they want a mechanic they have to go to Lake Maynard. I've always enjoyed getting my hands dirty and messing with engines. It'll be fun to be in my own motor pool all day."

"Glad it's you, not me. I freaked out when my little bro stole my battery a couple weeks before I got home. I was so mad. I sat and cried in my car when it wouldn't start at Fort Bronson."

"You should have called me. I'd have helped."

"Oh, Harry did." Ann drained the last of her coffee and stood. "It was right after I started working there when I couldn't get a teaching job for a while. And I straightened out Jack when I got home that night."

"Good thing you had time to calm down and didn't kick his butt," Derek said.

"Yeah, I'd never have heard the end of that. He's my step-mother's baby and we all know better than to mess with her."

"He should have served." Derek drawled. "If he had, maybe his older sis wouldn't be a better man than he is."

She smiled and the tension in her face melted away. "You're good for my ego, Waller. Let me get the list of presents I want for Devon, and you can start shopping for me. I can't expect Ginger to get them when my little angel is with her. If you have any issues, Kyra and Mindy will help resolve them."

"That works for me," Derek said.

CHAPTER SIX

Sitting in his recliner in front of the TV, Nick had chugged three beers when he got home. The rest of the six-pack sat within reach on the coffee table. He dozed off in the middle of the first *Die Hard* movie, waiting for Bruce Willis to wreak havoc after a stream of commercials. Shivering, Nick woke to a blaring version of Boris Karloff singing, *'You're a mean one, Mister Grinch!'* while the holiday cartoon played.

What happened? I wasn't asleep that long. He blinked and grabbed for the remote, but it wasn't on the arm of his chair any longer. *Where is it? Did it fall on the floor?* Nick felt around beside him but didn't find the remote on the chair cushion. He leaned over and checked the beige carpet.

"Looking for this? Too bad, too sad. I love watching this show with my kids and singing this song with them. How many times did we see it when we were their age?"

Nick stared at the man lounging on the couch across from

him, the TV remote beside the stranger. Not really staring at him, but more looking through him. Another ghost dressed in camos and combat boots. "What the hell are you doing here? How did you get into my house? I locked the door."

"How do you think? I floated through the wall. I'm dead, fool. Locked doors don't keep out ghosts. Marley warned you I'd be along."

"That was a sick joke."

"Wow, it's like what John Wayne always said, 'Life is hard and it's harder when you're stupid.' Come on, Nick. Let's go see Baker City in all its yesterday glory."

"What?"

"I'm the *Ghost of Christmas Past*. Move your lazy civilian butt, asshat."

Despite his protests, before Nick knew it, they wandered the snow-covered streets of their hometown. A giant evergreen festooned with strings of lights, tinsel garlands and multi-colored bulbs stood in front of the city hall while people in old-time clothes gathered for the tree-lighting ceremony. Nick remembered the building burned down twenty years ago when he was a teenager. It wasn't replaced because Baker City didn't have the money and his dad, a local banker, refused to loan the needed funds to the town council.

Tonight, it didn't matter. Reverend Thompson, the father of the current minister, led the citizens in a series of traditional holiday carols. Nick slowly recognized the young soldier conducting the high school orchestra from Lake Maynard as Smitty O'Sullivan who was in charge of the Baker City school board now. Applause and cheers rang out when the glorious lights on the tree brightened the winter night.

"Come on. Let's go." The ghost standing next to Nick gestured toward the church. "We have a lot to see and do before the Christmas Eve parade and the kids' party at the church. We can't be late to practice for the program at school, or Mrs. O'Sullivan will have us cleaning erasers for weeks."

"Baker City doesn't do any of those things anymore."

"It's why I'm the *Ghost of Christmas Past*, idiot. Shake a leg."

That was the strangest dream he'd had in years, Nick thought the next morning. He rose to his feet, picked up the remains of the six-pack, and carried the beer to the fridge. While he put on a pot of coffee, flashes of by-gone holidays flashed through his mind. Why did he think the season had always been horrible? It wasn't after his parents divorced and he and his sisters spent Christmas with his mother and her family or his dad's relatives most years.

Memories of visiting Santa at the mercantile, dressing up their dog and cat in costumes and waiting for their pets to see the jolly old elf, homemade hot chocolate when they frosted cookies at Janine O'Connell's house preparing for the annual cookie exchange, ice-skating on a pond outside of town, helping young Reverend Tommy set up a creche at the church. For the first time, Nick wondered why his father hated Christmas and did his best to wreck it for everyone.

Why am I following in his footsteps when he isn't one of my favorite people?

❄

It was still dark when Kyra dressed quietly and eased out of the apartment. She spotted Mindy's Ford Explorer coming up the driveway and went to meet her friend. Once in the passenger seat, Kyra buckled her seatbelt before she eyed the older woman. "Okay, what's first on the agenda? Please tell me it's the nearest espresso stand in Lake Maynard."

"You know it." Mindy turned her rig around and headed for the highway. "We're picking up Derek Waller at the Colter place on the way. I figure we'll put him to work hauling packages from the different stores to the parking lot. Did you and Debbie discuss a budget?"

"Yes, and she gave Trina permission to go through the attic at the house and find the boxes of decorations we already have for the barns. She and Jassy will do it right after chores."

"Talk to me." Mindy's attention remained on the highway. "Why is Jacinth Sweeney with Trina? Who is taking care of her grandpa, Dwight? He's a mean old bugger and she's the only one who has the patience to put up with him. She did even before he promised to leave the old Sweeney homeplace to her."

"She's on hiatus for at least the weekend." Kyra luxuriated in the warmth of the heated seat. "I have high hopes she'll let me write up an employment contract before she returns to her care-taking duties and insist the rest of the Sweeneys sign off, so she inherits the ranch. It needs to be in writing, notarized and filed with the county. The same goes with Dwight's last will and testament. That geriatric misogynist has decided once again she's replaceable by a man and he's found a new one to take over the ancestral homestead."

"It never works out for him, so I'd think Dwight could learn that." Mindy signaled and turned left onto a secondary road. "About the time he has to cook his own meals, prep his own meds, clean his place, do his laundry, feed his livestock, and handle the ranch maintenance, he'll call Jassy and order her to come home. Please tell me that you and Trina absconded with her cell phone."

"We didn't have to. Trina says Jassy threw it at him and told him to hire a new servant when he said it didn't matter that he promised her the old Sweeney farm forever. He's leaving it to the new foreman if one of the Sweeney males doesn't take it over. Miracle Stable doesn't open until after lunch, so Trina told me they're making a quick run into Lake Maynard. Jassy's taking her money out of the ranch account and getting a new phone. She told Dwight he can pay his way because she's done supporting the place."

"Now, I want to know how the rest of the Sweeney clan took her declaration of independence." Mindy parked in front of the large log cabin, and they waited for Derek to join them. "I'm pretty sure they weren't supportive because none of them want to take her place or look after Dwight and the hundred-acre, hardscrabble farm."

"You've got it." Kyra saw Derek approaching and hastily finished the topic. "They told Jassy to get over her snit and stay with him. It's not a big deal if he's passed her over for the new foreman and nobody appears to understand how devastated she feels."

"Oh, they understand all right. They just don't want to be under the proverbial elephant or serve as the family scapegoat. She needs to send someone to get her clothes, her dog, her cats, and her horses once she has a place or he'll guilt-trip her into reconsidering." Mindy smiled at Derek when he opened the door behind hers. "Good morning. Next stop is the espresso stand. If you tell us, you don't drink coffee, we're leaving you here."

He chuckled. "I can't live without it. When we're at the fort, I always go over to Colter's office for refills because Ann trained him to make a decent brew."

"And she learned how when she was working for my cousin at his café during one of her first jobs." Mindy followed the circular drive back to the road. "And now, let's discuss the kind of presents you're planning to buy for the kids, tweens and teens, Kyra. What suggestions did Debbie make? Do you have a list of what we need to find?"

While he listened to the conversation about decorations and presents at the barn, Derek wondered what they'd been discussing before he joined them. He'd 'hurry up and wait'. It wouldn't be the first time he opted for patience to win the game and learn what was really happening. A coffee stop later, they arrived at the mall. He followed them into the first department store where a greeter handed them coupons and gestured to a table containing free doughnuts and pastries telling them to help themselves.

"Okay, let's do it." When she finished the last bite of an old-fashioned cruller, Mindy grabbed a cart. "We need lots of red and gold tinsel garlands, decorative bells, reindeer, candles, candy canes, stockings, wreaths, snow globes, and angels."

"Is all that going in the barns?" Derek followed her. "What do the horses think of it?"

"Some of it goes in the lunch-room." Kyra tagged behind them, a maple bar in one hand and her mocha cup in the other. "We only put the non-toxic holiday stuff near the stalls. We also need gift wrap and ribbon, not just for the presents under the tree. We decorate with it."

They obviously had a routine derived from past experience. When the first cart was full, he found a second one. To take advantage of the BOGO deals, Kyra added assorted boxes of chocolate on the way to the cash register. Once they'd checked out, he was sent off to the SUV with the purchases and told where he'd find them in the next store.

It had everything a cowgirl or cowboy might want from display racks of outdoor clothes, gloves, riding boots, barn boots and equestrian helmets to the left. Shelves of gifts and souvenirs, including greeting cards on several spinner racks took up the front right corner. He found Kyra and Mindy sorting through grooming equipment for the horses. The new cart already held brightly colored lead lines, and bottles of horsy hair conditioner.

"Don't you also need shampoo?" Derek asked, enjoying the show when Kyra snagged two round, purple rubber things with teeth before another shopper, tossing them into the cart.

The question earned a scornful look from a petite, dark-haired woman assessing giant hairbrushes. "Baths and horses don't go together in the winter unless you have a way to totally dry them, so they don't catch cold."

"I didn't know that," Derek told her. "It's the first weekend I've been near horses."

"You're doing fine." Kyra smiled at him and held up a pink, rubber object that matched the purple ones she'd already found. "This is called a currycomb. It's used to bring dirt and loose hair to the surface of the coat and when it's pretty, a kid is more enthusiastic about using it to clean the horse."

"Really?" Derek pointed to a tote-box containing a variety of brushes on a nearby shelf. "Why don't you just grab a few sets of those?"

"Because it's expensive and the kids won't use all of them." Mindy gestured to one of the wire contraptions. "Plus, they don't need wire curries most of the time. With climate change, we don't have as much mud as we used to see in the olden days. When he was younger, my horse used to roll in it and was a complete mess when he came into the barn from the pasture."

"Sonora still tries to do that," Kyra said. "Trina and I groom him before you visit. He and my horse, Ebony always compete for the Mud Monster of the month title at Miracle."

"No wonder you and Trina are my favorite people," Mindy teased. She turned a warm smile on the brunette near the end of the aisle. "You're Amarillo Hawke, right? How many horses do you have?"

"It's Amie Ransom now. My husband wants to get our daughter a pony for Christmas and my sister-in-law offered to let us keep it at her place, but that can wait a while."

Mindy glanced at Kyra. "Do we have any ponies wanting Santa to bring them kids?"

"Not really." Kyra's smile didn't touch her gray eyes. She turned slightly to face Amarillo. "The new owner of Miracle Stable is expanding the programs to keep all of the ponies and horses busy in the off-season too. I don't think she plans to sell any of them, but I could take your number and have Debbie call you when she's back in town."

"Not needful." Amarillo's friendliness was just as plastic. "Maria rides with Darla at Painted Pony Park. It's closer to our house, and we'll keep the pony there until we're ready to take it to Heather and Durango."

"Makes good sense." Mindy scanned the two younger women before she urged Kyra in the opposite direction, signaling for Derek to follow them. "Happy holidays to you and yours, Amie."

"Same to you," Amarillo called.

Mindy waited until they were out of earshot. "What was that about, Kyra? We never turned down sales to good homes before, and you know as well as I do that Heather McElroy is a fantastic horse trainer. If she was looking after Amarillo's pony —"

"I cleaned up after Amie's antics too many times when I worked for her father," Kyra said, her tone low and deadly. "Let's agree to disagree on the subject, Mindy."

"All right. We'll talk about it later."

By the set of Kyra's jaw and the stiffness in her shoulders, Derek doubted there would ever be a conversation. Apparently, the topic was off the table, and it made him wonder what happened. He had a lot to learn about Kyra O'Neill. It was only

0900 hours on Friday morning. It didn't sound like she'd spent her entire life teaching horseback riding and managing a stable. What had she done with her life?

He had three days to play detective and complete his personal sitrep. He'd invite her to dinner tonight and see what there was to see. He looked forward to the adventure.

CHAPTER SEVEN

Newt O'Leary waved at Moises from the reserved corner booth as soon as he entered the cocktail lounge at Pop's Café on Friday morning. "I got a problem, young feller."

"What is it?" Moises sat down and gave the older ghost his undivided attention. "You're supposed to haunt Nick MacGillicudy tonight. Do I need to find someone else to be the *Ghost of Christmas Present*?"

"Oh, hell no! I'm looking forward to giving that boy a come-uppance. No, that's not it." Newt shook his head and rubbed a grizzled jaw. "What am I s'posed to show him? Zeke took him all over town and they saw the way we did Christmas forty some years ago. Folks barely have their decorations up today."

"That's true." Mayor O'Connell frowned thoughtfully. "You might take him to the cemetery, and he'd see the little, decorated trees on the graves. Virginia Thompson has the middle and high school kids putting those around today."

"And Twila Garvey posted signs for the Gingerbread House contest she's sponsoring all over Baker City. Janine O'Connell is talking about starting up her holiday cookie exchange again, but she hasn't committed to it yet." Florence MacGillicudy drifted closer. "Good to have those back. Couldn't you show what people were doing last year, Newt?"

"That's a good idea," Moises agreed. "One of my teachers used to say the "present" depends on what kind of answer you wanted, a literal, philosophical, mathematical, or biological one."

"I'll be telling you to use the literal one, Moises," Doireann O'Sullivan announced, coming to a stop beside Florence. "I'd say, "present" means a time that takes place continuously. Some folks call the Cenozoic era, the present era because it has been happening for 70 million years."

"That means "present" can be as long or short as you imagine, Newt." Moises slid out of the booth to his incorporeal feet. "Now, I need to find someone to be the *Ghost of Christmas Future*, and the ladies are waiting to help me choose the right woman for the job. Give me a sitrep about what you did with Nick later."

"I'll meet you here," Newt agreed and glanced at the mayor. "All right, O'Connell. Let's strategize."

Leaving the two older ghosts to talk, Moises went across the room with the previous school-teacher and the one-time farmer. Other women clustered around a long table and Moises nodded greetings to them. He spotted Raven Driscoll-Barlow taking names and glanced at her.

"What do we know?"

"Well, first we have to decide if this specter is going to talk or not or just scare the whiz out of Nick MacGillicudy." Raven gestured to the dark TV over the bar, and it came to life. She proceeded to stream several adaptations of the story, ranging from classic cartoons to newer versions. In many of them, the *Ghost of Christmas Future* was revealed as a dark, terrifying figure in a long cloak who escorted Ebenezer Scrooge from one dismal place to another, culminating in a ghastly scene at a graveyard.

"Silence can be intimidating," Moises mused. "Let's vote on the best way to horrify Nick. He has it coming and we want our last ghost to make a real impression on him."

When they returned to Miracle Riding Stable, Trina came to greet them accompanied not only by her sister, but also by Jason and Carol, the two seventeen-year-olds who worked most weekends. Jason waved a staple gun. Amused, Kyra handed him a bag filled with tinsel garlands. "Spread them out. We want them around each of the main doors on the barns and on all the gateposts. Leave the stalls for the boarders and students to decorate."

"You got it." Jason, a stocky, blond guy, headed off to complete his task. "I'll be back for another assignment."

"Thanks for the warning." Carol glanced at Mindy and Kyra. "Jassy helped me put the plastic candy canes and wreaths together for the pasture gates and we've tied them in place. What's next?"

"When I talked to her last night, Debbie said she'd ordered

trees from the mercantile," Kyra said. "Did you find the cowboy decorations we use for them, Trina?"

"Yes, and they're waiting in the lunch-room. When will the trees arrive?"

"I'll call Maxine Garvey and ask if they've been delivered to the store." Kyra turned to Jacinth. "I saw your pickup. Do you want to get them?"

The slender redhead nodded. "Sure. Who wants to come with me?"

"I will," Derek winked at her. "This is one of those rare times when I volunteer, so I guess you gals should make a note of it."

"Don't worry. We will," Mindy told him. "And we also won't share it with the vets around here. We don't want to ruin your rep."

"I appreciate that."

They spent the rest of the afternoon sprucing up the ranch for the holiday. Derek Waller had many likeable qualities, Kyra thought as they strung multi-colored, outdoor lights around the large, trail-riding corral and on the round pen. She wasn't the only one who had that opinion. Jassy had chattered away to him when they brought in the evergreens. He'd helped her place them in washtubs near the lunch-room, the office, the barn manager apartment and even on Debbie's back porch, adding dirt as needed. He'd seen to it they had water and promised to come back to plant them on New Year's Day.

He assisted Carol with the big plastic candy canes that went along the driveway. He listened to her sad tale of woe about a recent breakup with her boyfriend who'd traded the curvy brunette in for a skinny cheerleader. The drama was news to Kyra who'd wondered why the girl lost her smile, but Carol had it back, saying Derek called her 'ex' a stupid loser. Later, he and Jason mucked stalls together, sharing favorite football stories.

"I think you've found a keeper." Mindy filled water tubs while Kyra cleaned stalls. "Count your blessings. He's a good guy."

"I'm not interested." Kyra scooped another pile of horse manure. "Yes, he's been very helpful today, but it's temporary. He's just here for the weekend."

"Seattle isn't that far away, and you don't work twenty-four, seven. You could visit him, Kyra O'Neill."

"I could, but you're forgetting about Nick."

"I'm not, but I wish you would, sweetheart." Mindy moved to the next stall. "He's a Mr. Make-Do and you deserve a real man. Just think about it."

Kyra finished cleaning the stall and added clean shavings. "I will when you do. You're not part of the *Over the Hill Gang* yet."

"Honey, when you've had the best, the rest aren't worth your time." Mindy laughed. "If and when I find somebody who is more than a patch on my late husband's blue jeans, I'll let him bring me flowers. Thought I might meet someone on that singles cruise to Alaska last month, but the women outnumbered the men, and none of the guys sparked my interest."

Kyra nearly said nobody had brought her a bouquet or a box of chocolate in years. It wasn't Nick's style. He occasionally tossed in a few bucks when they went to dinner, but he'd never even given her a greeting card for her birthday. *Wow, I'm being pathetic tonight. Get over it, Kyra O'Neill. If you want candy, go to the mercantile and buy a box.*

Between the plastic candy canes on either side of the long driveway and bright lights twinkling on the corrals, Miracle Riding Stable looked festive. Derek sauntered toward the parking lot where Mindy waited. He saw her talking to Jassy, the young redhead who'd brought in the assortment of trees with him. He left them to it and went in search of Kyra. He found her in the office.

He enjoyed her smile. "Wondered if you'd join me for supper. Jassy tells me that Petrocelli's is a good Italian restaurant in Lake Maynard."

"They're always super busy on Friday nights. We'd need a reservation."

"Not too tough." He pulled out his cell phone. "I bet I can handle it."

She stared at him, obviously bewildered by the idea. "I'd have to shower and change."

"Me too. Shall I pick you up in an hour?"

"Why me, Waller?"

"Let's see. Because you're smart and sassy and you kick my ass at pool. That's a tough combination to beat, O'Neill. I haven't seen anyone in years who could."

"Okay, but only dinner. I'm not jumping in the sack with you on a first date."

"Not yet. Actually, tonight will be our fourth."

"No way!" Kyra shook her head. "How do you figure?"

"The first date was dessert and drinks on Wednesday. I helped in the barns yesterday and you joined us for dinner and that was our second date. We spent today together—number three and now, dinner —"

"Wow, sounds like someone's keeping track." Kyra pointed toward the door. "Guess you better get moving if we want to make the restaurant before midnight."

"Sounds fair." Derek left the office and strolled to the waiting vehicles. He held the driver's door to the SUV for Mindy, then walked around to the passenger side. "Hope I didn't keep you waiting long."

"No." She started the engine. "Jassy and I were talking about her renting a cabin at the dude ranch where I live, but she wasn't super enthused because Nighthawke Security has their headquarters in one of the other buildings."

"Why does it matter?"

"Because her grandfather opted to have one of their mercs take over the family homestead."

"That won't last." Derek buckled his seatbelt. "He'll leave on a mission before long."

"How do you figure?" Mindy drove toward the road. "He hasn't said anything about it."

"Contractors make more money out of CONUS than they do stateside." Derek shrugged. "I had offers, but I didn't take them. When I was in combat with them, I saw too many freaking *Charlie Foxtrots*, cluster-f—" He stopped. "I'm supposed to watch my potty-mouth now that Colter has a kid. He says I'm in train-ing, so I don't screw up when he and Ann add to their family and I'm the assigned godfather."

"Well, if you're around Kyra's students, you'll definitely want to be careful." Mindy frowned. "I wonder if Ann would let Jassy board some horses at their place."

"Won't know until you ask."

"That's fair."

At the Colters' log cabin, they saw Devon playing in the front yard with her half-grown collie mix, Shadow, along with a slightly older blue-gray and brown dog. Mindy parked safely in the drive, eyeing the trio. "It looks like Ann already got Jassy's heeler. Let's go check out the gossip."

"I'll catch up on it later." Derek headed for the house. "I'm picking up Kyra in forty-five minutes and we're going to dinner in Lake Maynard."

"I'm impressed." Mindy followed him. "How did you talk her into that?"

Derek shrugged. "If you don't ask, you don't get an answer."

"She's been dating—"

"A real asshat. I know. He stood her up on Wednesday night and luckily, I was there to tell her not to waste her time on him."

"All right!" Mindy pumped her arm in the air. "We've been saying that forever. Of course, if you hurt her, you're a dead man."

"Well, I'll have lots of company. Colter tells me there's tons of ghosts in Baker City."

❄

Once they'd cleaned the barns and fed the horses their supper on Friday, Kyra headed for the shower. Trina had agreed to look after Debbie's pets and Jassy left to settle into her new home in the ranch-hand cabin at Ann and Harry's place. Kyra decided to dress more casually than she had on Wednesday night at Pop's. She opted for coffee-colored corduroy pants and a cream print blouse with bucking broncos that were the same color as the jean-style slacks. A brown leather belt and decorator silver western buckle emphasized her waist, still slender despite the fact that she was almost forty.

Okay, she told herself. She had two years to go so it was time to quit acting older than her age. With that thought in mind, she chose her favorite cowgirl blossom boots. She usually saved them for line dancing on Saturday nights since the two-inch heels were too high for horseback riding. Her favorite horsy earrings and matching necklace finished off the outfit. Fresh makeup and she left her hair to hang free.

Trina tapped on the door. "Time to stop primping. Derek just arrived. He cleans up good."

"Thanks." Kyra left the bathroom. "Are you okay home alone?"

"I'm not." Trina gestured to the two dogs following them toward the living-room. "They came with me from the big house. We're going to junk out in front of Hallmark movies. Derek said you'd bring home my fave lasagna for me. Remember, it's the cheesy and meat sauce one. Salad dressing on the side and keep the garlic bread separate so it doesn't get soggy. Jassy brought back pie from Pop's Café because I'd missed out on hers yesterday, so I'm good for dessert."

"Nice." Kyra smiled at Derek who waited near the door of their apartment. He'd changed to black jeans and one of the dark military-style sweaters that matched his eyes. If anyone had ever told her she'd find a man with a receding hairline attractive, after being with a hot guy like Nick MacGillicudy, she'd have told them to get a life. However, there was something special about a dinner date with another adult, especially one who offered to buy a complete supper for her room-mate, no strings attached.

"Are you ready?" Derek asked.

"Definitely." Kyra collected her suede, fringed jacket from the back of her recliner. "We won't make a late night of it, Trina. There's plenty of work to do tomorrow because Debbie and the girls aren't here to help."

"Okay, but Jassy will be over in time for breakfast. She plans to take out trail rides with me," Trina said. "She wants you to do that employment contract for her in case Grandpa gets his head on straight."

"No worries. I'm happy to help."

Derek waited until they were in his truck before he asked. "Why do you know about contracts?"

"I was a lawyer in one of my former lives," Kyra said. "I decided to reclaim my soul, so I walked away five years ago and came here."

"Sounds like there's more to the story." Derek started the engine. "Are you going to share it?"

"Possibly, if there's wine in my future and if you share a few dirty details about your past." Kyra fastened her seatbelt. "Like when you decided the Army was the life for you?"

He shrugged and started down the winding driveway toward the one-lane bridge over Cedar Creek. "My mother died when I was twelve and I spent the next two years in one foster home after another —"

"Where was your father?"

"Long gone. The state tried tracking him down, but it didn't do any good. They couldn't find his family either. When I was fourteen, I was homeless and living hand to mouth on the streets. One of the local recruiters used to let me bunk in the back of the office on cold nights and fed me leftovers from his lunch and dinner or sent me to the local fast-food place to bring back burgers for us."

"And he convinced you to enlist when you turned eighteen?"

"Didn't take much convincing. When you're promised three squares a day, decent new clothes, a roof over your head plus a living wage and you're assured nobody will put their hands on you—" He shrugged. "Well, I signed the papers. It wasn't necessary to finish high school or have a GED because the Army was desperate for cannon fodder."

She studied his features in the dimly lit pickup cab. "You weren't eighteen, were you?"

"I had a birth certificate that said I was."

"And I know where you can buy those on the streets of Seattle, not to mention a half-dozen other cities." She shook her head, amazed by his courage. She couldn't imagine volunteering to join the military when she was barely a teenager. "You were a survivor even then, weren't you?"

"Takes one to know one." He flashed a grin her way. "Tell me why you went to law school."

"I was going to save the world." She heaved a sigh. "Turned out it was a bigger project than I thought it'd be."

"It always is."

CHAPTER EIGHT

Back from visiting his Army buddies at the military hospital near Fort Clark, Moises Pride hummed his mother's favorite holiday song on his way into the cocktail lounge on Friday afternoon. Yes, he needed a little Christmas right now. *Candles in the window, carols at the spinet.* He had a meeting with Newt O'Leary to learn what the old hardware store owner intended to do with Nick MacGillicudy later tonight.

Linda MacGillicudy had tacked sparkling gold, red and green garlands around the room, from corner to corner near the ceiling. A flocked artificial tree stood in the corner near the doors to the restrooms. It hadn't been decorated yet. Moises glimpsed clusters of mistletoe waiting on the bar. Meantime, he checked the various entrances and exits.

Yup, the woman needed his help, and so did romance in Baker City. He knew exactly where to hang the plants and hopefully, everyone would have a kissing good time this year. No snow yet, Moises thought, but Santa needed to get a move on and start loading up the sleigh in front of the feedstore.

While he was helping Jacinth Sweeney transport Christmas trees, he'd mentioned wanting to take Kyra to dinner that night. Jassy had told him Petrocelli's Italian restaurant was a popular choice not only for people who lived in Lake Maynard, but also those from Baker City. Since he planned to move to the area in the near future, Derek decided it was time to check out the place. The parking lot was almost full when he pulled into a slot, so he was glad he'd made a dinner reservation.

Their table wasn't quite ready. The hostess suggested they wait in the cocktail lounge for a few minutes, and she'd call them. When he asked, Kyra agreed. The two of them found stools at the bar and ordered glasses of wine. Once the bartender moved down to take care of other patrons, Derek focused on Kyra. "Your turn. What's your family like?"

"Mercenary as hell." She sipped the red wine. "As soon as I didn't have the big bucks from my law career to spend on them or their kids, they didn't have time for me. I go low to no contact depending on the situation. If one of my parents ends up in the hospital, I visit, but Mindy and I are closer."

"Were you upset when she sold the stable?"

"Oh, Mindy had it listed for years, but nobody was really interested. Her relatives thought they'd inherit and be able to turn the place into a gravel pit. When Debbie Ramsey came along, they negotiated for a while. Mindy wanted to be sure all the horses would continue to have a good home and none of them would be hauled off to the nearest slaughterhouse in Canada."

"Was that likely to happen?"

Kyra shook her head. "Not with Debbie. It had with some other potential buyers. We knew Debbie was the right person when she wanted to know what stalls were available for her personal horses. She and Mindy barely closed on the deal before Hobby and Wonder arrived around the Fourth of July."

"Is that a busy time of year?" Derek signaled the bartender for refills. "Most of the kids are out of school and people are looking for things to do."

"Horses and fireworks don't mix, so we always shut down for a week or so. Debbie showed up and stayed for ten days to help because the horses spent most of their time in the stalls."

"Was that a surprise?"

"Yes, but a bigger one was when she moved to the stable in August. She hadn't mentioned she was married or had kids and she arrived with her two daughters. Then, we found out her three stepsons attend WSU in Pullman. Finally, her niece came to stay because Debbie's brother was preparing to leave for Afghanistan." Kyra finished her wine. "They're great kids."

"And you like them."

"What's not to like? The girls take lessons from me after school and they're always willing to help with horse chores. When the boys are home from college, they jump in too. And the major, Debbie's husband, is a good guy. He was the one who suggested she promote me to management and give me a raise."

While they enjoyed their second glasses of wine, he learned

more about the day-to-day operations of the stable. In addition, Kyra shared that Linda MacGillicudy, who helped her father run the café in Baker City adopted Debbie's biological son, Dray, when he was an infant. It wasn't a one-sided conversation. When she asked open-ended questions, he talked more about growing up in the military and the different parts of the world where he'd been stationed. A short time later, they entered the dining room, and the hostess led them toward a secluded booth.

Halfway there, a tall, dark-haired man in cowboy attire of jeans, a western shirt, and a denim jacket spotted them. Something about the way he carried himself screamed prior service. He approached. "Kyra O'Neill, right?"

"Yes." Kyra's tone was formal and distant. "You're Bendigo Hawke, aren't you?"

He nodded, concern etched on his rugged features and landing in the cobalt eyes. "Do you know where Jacinth Sweeney went?"

"Yes." Kyra stepped closer to Derek. "Why?"

"I need to talk to her."

"I'll pass the word," Kyra said, "but that's it. I may not be actively practicing law anymore, but I always respect my clients' confidentiality." She glanced at Derek. "Let's eat."

"Definitely." He cupped her elbow, and they followed the hostess.

Once they were seated, Kyra eyed him. "You didn't share anything about Jassy either."

"I'm no lawyer, but I've been through a few *Charlie-Foxtrots* or cluster-fu--over the years." He shook his head. "I got the word from Devon that you don't care for 'potty-mouth', so I'll control the urge to say a few other inappropriate things."

Kyra laughed. "Oh, I know all that vocabulary and I've been known to utilize it when I feel it's required. I don't use those words around the kiddoes, because I have to set a good example for them, the tweens, and the teens. Don't sanitize your language for me."

"Well, that's a relief."

Friday night, Nick checked the windows and doors of his one-bedroom trailer. Everything was locked up tight. He'd also closed the gates off the road, figuring his dad, his mom and sisters had keys to the property so it wouldn't keep them out, but it should deter any other trespassers. He microwaved dinner and ate it, washing down the pasta with a soda rather than a beer. He drank too much last night, which was why he'd had such a crazy dream. Tonight, he'd play it smart.

Rather than crashing in the recliner, he headed for the king-size bed in his room. He decided to stay in his jeans and T-shirt, not sleep in his shorts like usual. Propping up a pillow, he selected one of the old Louis L'Amour western novels his grand-father left him. He'd read a while, not turn on the small TV in the bedroom for a distraction. The place was quiet when he finally shut off the light two hours later. It was safe, he thought. Time to catch some Z's.

It didn't feel like he'd been sleeping very long when a deep voice roared. "Wake up, young feller. We got places to go and things to do!"

"No way!" Nick sat up and glimpsed a burly figure lurking in the doorway. "Who the hell are you?"

"The *Ghost of Christmas Present* and I ain't talking about gifts. Move your lazy butt, boy. Time to mosey and see what there is to see tonight."

"What if I don't?"

The stranger came closer, and a cold wind whipped the blankets off the bed. "You don't want to know what else I can do. I been dead a lot longer than Zeke Garvey and I have more power than he does. Let's go!"

Nick stumbled to his feet. "Where are you taking me?"

"All around the town." The ghost pointed to Nick's boots. "You're gonna want those, sonny. So, shove them on and let's move."

Tonight, he didn't see the vintage decorations he had the night before. The town bakery had strings of icicle lights hanging from the eaves and around the windows. A large poster in one of the bay windows announced an upcoming ginger-bread house contest for kids and adults. A few of the other businesses had started to decorate for the holiday. Someone—he knew it was his sister, Dominique—had painted winter scenes on the large windows at the café.

The mercantile had a row of living evergreens lined up near the front of the building along with a selection of cut ones. When Nick asked why nobody would steal them, his ghostly escort reminded him it was Baker City, and nobody wanted to answer to their dead ancestors. That made sense in an odd sort of way. Over at the feedstore, Summer O'Neill had an antique sleigh waiting for the upcoming winter snow. It wasn't full of presents yet, but Nick remembered the former owner driving it around town to deliver gifts to needy families for their children.

At the church, they found Reverend Tommy tuning the piano while his wife, Virginia, and the choir director discussed the upcoming Christmas program. The three of them launched into a medley of classic holiday songs once the minister was ready to play them. Afterwards, Nick and his companion wandered through the cemetery to see little, potted trees on the individual graves.

"What happened to the town celebration?" Nick asked. "Why isn't there a big tree like the one that used to be in the center of Baker City? Where's the nativity scene?"

"We never did get the money to rebuild the town hall and they had their lawyers go after the Business Council the last time they tried to put up a creche," the ghost answered. "Your father and his buddy, Liam O'Leary also orchestrated a power struggle, so the city council and the living mayor quit ten years ago. It's left a void somebody had to fill, so we are along with the current business owners."

"That doesn't make any sense." Nick glanced at the chapel. "Reverend Tommy has a big yard in front of the church. He could pull the old nativity scene out of storage and refurbish it."

"He doesn't want to start a war during what's supposed to be a time of peace and joy. Come along. Let's go look at what other folks are doing."

"You're only showing me the positive side of things. What

about the people who argue and drink and fight with their relatives?"

"Contrary to what Herman and his minions think, there's enough sadness and anger in everybody's lives. The holidays are supposed to be a time when we brighten the dark days of winter, not when we start more trouble for one another. Your old man should have shared human kindness with you and your sisters, instead of teaching hatred and scorn. Let's go see what one amazing person does to counteract his poison."

They stopped outside the new real-estate office his younger sister bought last summer. Nick saw brilliant gold, green, blue, and red garlands intermingling with the string of holiday lights framing the doors and windows. Dominique MacGillicudy stood on the sidewalk while she painted a fat snowman on the largest pane of glass. Instead of her usual fashion diva attire, she wore old sweatpants, a sloppy flannel shirt over a skimpy tank-top and battered running shoes. Her golden blonde hair hung in a fat braid halfway down her back. Beside her, a radio played classic songs. She happily sang along, off-key as usual, about Santa bringing her ornaments from Tiffanys'.

Nick chuckled. She always made a big deal about Christmas. She told everyone in the family it was when she sold the most houses and cracked jokes about gathering all her sales staff around the cash register. Of course, it didn't explain why she paid out early holiday bonuses to those people when she was just the manager of the brokerage. Back then, she arranged to close the realty for two weeks in December. She closed a few days before Christmas Eve and reopened after New Years, which totally pissed off their father, Herman MacGillicudy.

Dominique always told him she'd worked hard all year and she was headed for Hawaii, or maybe New York City. She told him to call it her Christmas present. Maybe she had the right idea, Nick thought. He might try exiting stage left this year too! At least, then, he wouldn't be plagued by ghostly visitors.

Early Saturday morning, she was the first in the kitchen. Kyra put the coffee on to brew while she pulled their favorite muffin tops out of the refrigerator. Next came an assortment of fresh fruit, grapes, oranges, and apples. She glanced over her shoulder as Trina entered the room, followed by her older sister who'd just arrived.

Like her, the two redheads were dressed for Miracle Riding Stable success in jeans, sweatshirts, and lace-up boots. They'd also taken time to do hair and make-up. Well, all of them were professional horsewomen and knew appearances were what was important to the customers and more crucially to their parents who supplied the payments that supported the place.

"What's on the agenda today, Jassy?" Kyra focused on the part-time barn manager who usually worked on weekdays. "Are you helping us out here?"

"First, you have to tell us about your hot date last night," Trina said. "How was it?"

"Nice." The coffeepot gave its last gurgle and Kyra filled three cups. "Derek was a perfect gentleman."

"Sounds boring." Trina sat down at the table and reached for a lemon poppyseed muffin top. "I hope I never get so old I'm comfortable with that."

"Stuff it," Jacinth recommended. "Tell us more, Kyra. Did he kiss you?"

"No. Never even tried." Kyra wouldn't admit it'd disappointed her. She reminded herself she'd dated someone else off and on for the last five years. Of course, she didn't want some guy she barely knew trying to jump her bones. "And he won't be around today. He's helping Harry Colter with Christmas trees."

"I like Harry." Jacinth sipped her coffee. "I did even before Ann called and offered to pick up my critters and my clothes and —"

"What the hell?" Kyra blinked and stared at the younger woman. "How did Ann learn about any of this? Did you talk to her?"

"Nope." After sitting down across from her sister, Jacinth reached for an orange-cranberry muffin top. "She called me yesterday because several of the Sweeneys contacted her looking for me. They still consider she's part of the clan since she was married to Will Sweeney."

"So, what?" It was Kyra's turn to grab one of her favorite chocolate chip muffin tops. "He told me you hassled him after she left."

"It wasn't as if she had a choice." Trina narrowed her blue eyes. "He made it sound like his wife abandoned him and that's why he filed for divorce but the whole town knew he was whining because her Army Reserve unit shipped out and he had to 'daddy-up' and take care of their four-and-a-half-year-old daughter, Devon."

"And when Will posted a garage sale on the Internet, I didn't think anything of it because I knew he'd been fired again," Jacinth said. "I'm always on the hunt for hand tools for the Sweeney ranch, so I stopped by. I discovered he was selling all the household goods along with Ann's clothes."

"Wait a second." Kyra lifted a hand. "That isn't what he told me."

"Of course not." Trina took another bite of her muffin, chewed, and swallowed. "If he'd admitted he was the asshat Ann calls him, you wouldn't have felt sorry for him, and Will always loves to play the pity card. He needed you to represent him and help save his sorry butt during the divorce when Frank Madison went after him. Will wanted you to use your influence around town to find him jobs and loans."

"Next time I see him, I'm kicking his tail up one street and down the other in Baker City." Kyra fumed silently for a moment. "It didn't feel right, so I refused to help him with his divorce. I have my rep as a bitch to uphold, and I don't like liars. If I did, I'd have continued being a mouthpiece for Tex Hawke. Now, what's going on with Ann and Harry?"

"They went over to the Sweeney place and got my things and my animals," Jacinth said. "When Grandpa tried telling them I'd be back soon, Ann told him that he'd crapped on me one too many times. She ripped Bendigo Hawke a new one while she was there and said he had no business stealing my home when I was the only one who stepped up to help him instead of calling the Hawkes to fetch their drunken, stone-ass stupid relative."

"Tell me more." Kyra pulled out a chair and sat down at the

kitchen table. "We ran into him at Petrocelli's, but I didn't tell him where you were. Figured it wasn't my place to share it."

"Thanks." Jacinth drank some coffee. "Ann really stepped up for me. She offered me her ranch-hand cabin and when I got there last night, she and Devon had already scrubbed the place from top to bottom. Next time I work at Pop's, I'm telling Linda that her cleaning company has some stiff competition."

Kyra laughed. "How big is the place?"

"It's not huge, but it has two bedrooms. The bathroom is between them. I'll use one room as an office. Almost open concept because there isn't a wall between the kitchen and living-room, but it's comfortable. The pantry even has a washer and dryer, so I won't have to go to the laundry in Lake Maynard or use yours."

"What else?" Trina asked. "I can't wait to see it."

"Harry set up my TV and he'd already arranged for cable service to the cabin because he planned to hire someone to do maintenance or use it for guests. My horses were in their barn when I arrived, and Laredo brought over my dog, Rounder. He was playing with Devon and her pup."

"Sounds awesome," Kyra refilled their coffee cups. "Trina and I will be coming for lunch when Debbie gets back. Be sure we have your new cell number so we can text you."

"No worries." Another big smile. "They have Internet access because they need it for their jobs, so I was able to email all my clients about where to find their horses." Jacintha heaved a sigh. "I slept so well in that king-size bed. Rounder and I love it. Grandpa is real grumpy when he comes inside, and I didn't realize how stressed out I get when he yells at my dog or hollers at me to get up and fix his breakfast at the crack of dawn after I've worked the closing shift at Pop's cocktail lounge."

"Enjoy your hiatus," Kyra finished off her muffin top. "I'm serious about that contract. You can use it for your new clients too."

"I will." Jacinth nodded. "Harry said I could train horses at their place for as long as I wanted. They don't have an indoor arena yet, but they do have a round pen and Harry built a big outdoor corral last summer. My six whiners, or maybe I should say, 'whinniers' need to step up and learn to be real western Washington horses and work outside in the rain, snow, and mud. I'm good with it because Grandpa threw a fit when I wanted to buy an indoor arena, so the Sweeney place doesn't have one either."

Kyra eyed the pair. "I didn't know Ann or Harry had a trailer to haul horses."

"They don't. Ann borrowed her dad's," Trina said. "And Frank Madison told her that he'd already called Grandpa to give him a heads-up that since the Sweeneys didn't have room or time for Jassy in their lives, she was next on the list to be hired at Majestyk Morgans, Frank's breeding farm as soon as he has an opening."

"He pays tons of money, plus his help has really nice housing." Jacinth finished her muffin. "However, I'd be so busy there, I couldn't work here or at the dude ranch or run my own training business. It'd take some serious negotiation to keep my clients and their horses happy."

"He's very high maintenance too and his wife —" Trina shook her head. "I'm glad you turned him down."

"Not forever. Just for now. Things may change next spring when the dude ranch opens." Jacinth glanced at the clock. "We'd better hustle. There are horses to feed, and we'll have customers arriving in three hours."

"Hang on. I'm supposed to be the boss here." Kyra laughed and stood. She was glad Jacinth rescued herself. *It's a responsibility I don't have to take, and I have enough to do.*

Between classes, Kyra helped students enter the annual barn holiday contest. They'd decorate their favorite horses' stall doors. Prizes included discounts on spring and summer horse camps, riding lessons, and club memberships. During lunch, she felt her phone vibrate and pulled it out of her pocket to see a message from Derek inviting her to join him at Pop's Café that night.

After a moment, she accepted. It wasn't as if Nick was beating down the door. He hadn't even called to apologize for standing her up on Wednesday night. He was probably out with one of the sluts he'd found at Pop's last weekend. Okay, the girls undoubtedly weren't sleazy. They just didn't want a grown-up guy who was in it for the long haul and since Nick didn't do commitments, he'd found the kind of women he wanted. And she'd begun to realize it wasn't her!

Before her last lesson, she saw a late-model, white Cadillac pull into the parking lot. Shortly thereafter, a stocky man with neatly trimmed silver blond hair wearing a three-piece suit came toward her. Kyra recognized him as Herman MacGillicudy, Nick's father. She went to greet him. "Hello, Mr. MacGillicudy. How can I help you?"

"I'm looking for Nick. According to his schedule, he's supposed to be here today."

Kyra shook her head. "Not anymore. The new owner hired someone else to shoe the horses and he isn't due back until next week."

"Nick didn't tell me he'd been replaced." A polite smile appeared on Herman's ruddy face, but it didn't touch the pale, blue eyes. He handed Kyra a business card from the Lake Maynard bank he managed. "Would you ask the owner to call me?"

"Why?" Kyra tucked the card into her jeans. "Debbie Ramsey just bought the place. I don't think she's interested in selling it as a gravel pit."

"She can make that decision after she hears what I'm willing to pay." With another nod, Herman turned away. "Tell Nick to charge up his cell phone and call me."

"If I see him, I will." Kyra headed toward the arena. She didn't bother to tell Herman MacGillicudy it wasn't likely. She had work to do and passing on a message from such an asshat wasn't high on her priority list!

CHAPTER NINE

He'd done more than his share of physical labor during the last thirty years in the Army. Digging up small evergreens and wrapping the roots in burlap before they transported them to the barn took most of Saturday. Oddly enough, he enjoyed the adventure. He and Harry had time to talk about the logistics of the battalion's move to Fort Darby after New Years.

If they scheduled it correctly, they could have the reservists, what Derek still thought of as 'weekend warriors' do most of the work. Otherwise, it'd take weeks they didn't have to empty out the buildings at Fort Bronson. He'd miss his rooms at the old, ramshackle barracks. His new apartment had all the bells and whistles from an ensuite bathroom to a kitchenette and a sitting area in addition to the bedroom with a large closet.

Granted, once he retired in the near future, Harry would have the opportunity to use the suite on the nights he couldn't make it back to Baker City. Then again, he and Ann might appreciate the privacy on reserve weekends when they had a babysitter and thanks to her arrangement with Jacinth Sweeney, they wouldn't have to worry about what Ann referred to as 'critter care'. She'd said both sets of grandparents often argued about who'd look after Devon and that now included Harry's grandmother, plus the little girl had an ongoing invite to stay with her friends at the dude ranch.

Derek lined up the galvanized washtubs and helped move the trees, one spruce at a time, into them. He stretched out the hose, preparing to water them. "So, what are you doing about the family drama between the Sweeneys and the Hawkes?"

"Absolutely nothing." Harry shoveled dirt in the tubs to help hold the evergreens in place. "Ann says everyone in the Sweeney family takes little side-steps to avoid looking after the elders, and Dwight isn't as bad as his predecessors. Someone in each generation ends up being the sucker in charge, but it doesn't mean they get reimbursed financially. This time around, it was Jacinth. Getting screwed is part of the ongoing conflama."

"What about the Hawkes?"

"What about them?" Harry shrugged. "It will be interesting to see how they handle it when they hear Bendigo is inheriting the Sweeney place. He was around yesterday when Ann and I were there. Said he intended to have a sit-down with the old man and tell Dwight where the bear got in the buckwheat."

"Makes me wonder how he's going to resolve things with Jacinth. She's not willing to be the family doormat or scapegoat any longer."

"Good point." Harry lowered his shovel. "I'll let you share

that with the womenfolk who are determined to save her because I hate sleeping alone."

Derek laughed and switched off the nozzle at the end of the hose before heading toward the horses and their water tubs. "Shall we do chores now? I'm meeting Kyra at Pop's Café in two hours, and I don't want to be late."

"Let's do our best." Harry glanced toward the eight stalls and their equine inhabitants. "If we're not done in an hour, I'll get Devon, the best pooper-scooper to give me a hand."

When Derek arrived at the café, shortly after 1900 hours, seven o'clock at night, civilian time, he spotted Kyra coming toward him. She sizzled in a bright blue wrap-tie midi dress with short sleeves and a sash that fastened on the side. He reminded himself they'd only been seeing each other for a few days. Taking her to a motel in Lake Maynard to undress his own Christmas angel would be totally inappropriate. Wow, those tan spike heels made her long legs even sexier and he contemplated how she'd look in only the shoes—

Stop, Waller. You invited the woman to supper. Don't be a horndog!

When she smiled at him, he caught her hand and drew her close enough to kiss her cheek. "Glad you could make it."

"Me too." Another smile and she tucked her fingers in his. "I'd much rather have something here than more Thanksgiving leftovers."

"And I hoped you liked me."

"I do." She wrinkled her nose. "Okay, those are two words I promised never to use in a sentence."

He chuckled. "I won't hold you to them." He paused. "Yet."

"Thanks for the warning."

When they walked into the cocktail lounge, they were surprised by a couple kissing in the doorway. The pair broke apart and the woman laughed, pointing to the mistletoe attached to the beam overhead. "Don't waste the opportunity. Merry Christmas."

"Give me a break, Heather McElroy." Kyra sniffed. "You and your hubby never needed to use a parasitic plant that grows on trees and is spread through birds' feces to jump each other." She glared upward at the sprig of green. "And those berries are poisonous too."

"Good luck, pal." The tall, rugged behemoth put an arm around his woman's waist and guided her toward the lounge. "You're going to need it. Kyra O'Neill isn't what we'd call romantic."

"I make my own luck." Derek pulled Kyra against him. He didn't need mistletoe, but he wasn't going to ignore a holiday tradition that suited him. He lowered his head and his mouth claimed hers.

As soon as Moises drifted into the cocktail lounge Saturday night, he was surrounded by several concerned ghosts, all females. He glanced at Raven Driscoll-Barlow. "What's going on?"

"Nick MacGillicudy hasn't been home all day. He's nowhere in or near Baker City and it's Ling Zhao's turn to haunt him. What do we do?"

"We wait." Moises smiled at the diminutive Chinese woman who'd operated one of the first laundries in the town's early days while her husband worked in the silver mines. "He'll turn up. He hasn't moved away yet."

"Are you sure?" Ling tugged on the long black coat she wore. "I'm ready."

"I know." Moises gestured toward the reserved booth where Newt O'Leary and the mayor sat. "Let's go see what Newt did last night. He couldn't have scared him badly enough to vacate the premises for good."

The comment earned laughter from the women, and he followed them across the room. On the way, he spotted Kyra O'Neill and Derek Waller playing pool. "How are they doing?"

"Very well, if you consider the hot and heavy kiss under the mistletoe when they arrived three hours ago," Raven said. "Made me miss my guy and our Christmas two years ago. I jumped him so many times under our tree. He didn't complain."

"Why would he?" Moises asked gently. "I'll bet he wishes you were there to do it again."

"He's not the only one."

Nick MacGillicudy was exhausted after spending the last two nights with dead people who took him slogging through his hometown, overwhelming him with holiday nostalgia. A long drive to south Liberty Valley through non-stop holiday traffic today hadn't helped. Neither had the strong coffee he drank while he ate breakfast, lunch, and supper at chain restaurants near the freeway.

While he was in the area, he'd stopped by his mother's house and visited her. He didn't know his future plans so he couldn't share them but promised to call and drop by more often. He agreed to tell his sisters to do the same. Instead of making it all the way to Baker City Saturday night, he checked into a motel. Distantly, he remembered his grandparents telling him there were very few ghosts in Liberty Valley. The witches in the local covens didn't tolerate them. He didn't know if it was true or not, but a good night's sleep couldn't hurt. He had plans for the next day.

Nothing disturbed him and he slept deeply in short stretches. He still woke up when he heard semi-trucks roar on the highway. But thankfully, the dead remained where they belonged in Baker City. Sunday morning, he hit the shower before he dressed. He was on the road before daylight. A quick stop for gas provided the chance to grab a huge coffee and an awful sandwich that he barely managed to gag down while he drove north.

Nick reached Baker City in time to stop at the café for a real breakfast prior to church services. Pop gave him a long look when he sat at the counter instead of taking up space in a booth. "Morning. May I please have coffee and a stack of pancakes? Bacon on the side."

Pop nodded, wrote down the order and passed it to his daughter, Linda, working in the kitchen. Silence ensued while he filled a mug and slid it onto the counter, along with silverware wrapped in a paper napkin. "Are you all right, Nick? You don't sound like yourself, and you don't look too good either."

"I'm better than I was the past couple of nights. At least I got some sleep."

Bells rattled over the main door when it opened, then closed. Nobody entered the restaurant, and Pop glanced over his shoulder. "Stop that. The boy isn't doing any harm to me or mine. Let him have a meal in peace and quiet. The pancakes will be up in a minute. You want syrup or jam?"

"Syrup, please." In the middle of his meal, the door opened again, but this time a real, living woman entered the café, his youngest sister. Nick glanced at the petite blonde, in a tight-fitting sequined tank-top that emphasized her full breasts, sans bra as usual, and faded, glued-on, slashed jeans tucked into spike-heeled, bling covered, western boots. Her bright red lipstick matched her red fingernail polish. "What's going on, Veronika?"

"That's my question." She hiked up on the stool next to him. "Daddy's been hunting for you. He wants your latest report on the horse places he can get for their gravel."

"I told him before I'm not into being his spy."

"Then you better find somewhere else to live. He didn't pay for you to go to shoeing school for free."

"He didn't pay at all." Nick finished off his pancakes and had a last swallow of coffee. "The only paychecks that ever bounced were the ones he wrote me. And it made my name mud all over town when I passed on the pain with my debit card. I'm done being embarrassed and kicked out of the Baker City businesses. I quit."

"What?" Veronika widened big blue eyes, gaping at him. "You quit what?"

"I quit shoeing. I sold my equipment yesterday. I'll quit renting his place too. I'll get my stuff from the trailer later today. Most of the furniture is mine, so I'm taking it with me. I'll change the utilities tomorrow. And if you don't irritate me, I won't quit being your big bro. Call Mom. For some odd reason, she loves and misses you." Nick stood. "Don't ask me for any more money. Get it from Dad. You're his favorite chick right now."

"Where are you going?"

"To church. There are people I need to see." Nick picked up the check and waved at Pop. "Let me pay you now before Veronika takes the money and runs again. I'm done cleaning up her messes too."

"About time." Pop said as he approached. "You're amazing me today, Nick. I'm glad to see you're not a chip off your father's block. Your mother has class. Most of the O'Learys do. Keep acting like them, not him."

Veronika gasped, then glared at Nick. "How dare you call me a thief?"

"Because you are one. I've seen you do it time and again, not only to me. Mom used to call you out for stealing the tips she left for waitresses when we were kids and Dad just laughed about it. But I won't be like the pair of you. I'm changing. I suggest you try it before your sins come back and bite you in the butt."

❄

Kyra always attended church on Sunday morning, not because she was super religious. She wasn't, but she enjoyed Reverend Tommy's sermons and the chance to visit with her friends in town. True, she wasn't close to her family anymore, but that didn't mean she didn't talk to her parents and the rest of the O'Neill crew if they were polite and didn't demand cold, hard cash. Today, when she and Trina entered the building, they spotted Nick MacGillicudy talking to the minister.

"That's new." Trina elbowed Kyra. "Why do you think he's here? Is he looking for a handout?"

"I have no idea. We may find out." Kyra led the way to their favorite pew, and they slid into their usual seats. Before Nick joined them, Ann Barrett arrived with her husband, her daughter, Devon, and Derek. He co-opted the seat next to hers.

Kyra struggled to ignore the heat warming her cheeks when he put an arm around her. She shivered, remembering the kiss under the mistletoe the night before and the longer, steamier one when he walked her to her car. "I didn't expect to see you here today."

"Then you weren't paying attention when I said I'd see you tomorrow."

Kyra nearly admitted the truth. She'd been so caught up in his embrace she was lucky she recalled her own name. He was in civvies, the same ones he'd worn most of the weekend. Stonewashed jeans hugged long legs and a black sweater clung to broad shoulders, muscular arms, and a wide chest. He wasn't classically handsome like Nick, but she'd learned she preferred Derek's rugged good looks and the amusement that lit his dark gaze.

Kyra traced a line over his cheek, feeling a hint of stubble. She caught a whiff of lime aftershave. "Okay, I hate to say it when somebody's right, but unfortunately you are."

"I can go with that." He grinned at her. "Ann told me I have to behave myself and not tell any lawyer jokes in church or you'll kick my butt."

"I don't mind if they're actually funny." She glanced past him to the other woman. "I thought you'd be pissed at me because I gave your ex-husband a referral to a different attorney."

"If you hadn't, he'd have found someone on the Internet." Ann beamed, a sunshine smile. "Besides, if Will hadn't done the 'Dear John' thing when I was in Afghanistan, I wouldn't have Harry. And Jassy told us that you'd never represent liars, so that makes you a winner in our books."

"She raved about the two-bedroom cabin you and Harry gave her for the duration," Kyra said. "She told Trina and me all about the way you and Devon cleaned it for her, that you're going to beat Linda at her housekeeping game."

Ann laughed. "Not hardly. It was good practice. I haven't GI'd a place since Harry had my team muck out our company HQ last spring."

"What's GI'd mean?" Kyra asked, baffled by the term.

"Cleaning like sojers do," Devon explained. "Mama told me I had to get all the dirt out of the floor, or I'd be using a tooth-brush on the gross spots in the bathroom. 'Cept it's not the one I use at bedtime to brush my teeth."

"Good decision," Derek told her. "I bet Jassy will do as good a job keeping her place neat and tidy."

Devon nodded enthusiastically. "Yup. I shared when Shadow

and me took Rounder home. If your room isn't super spick and span when Mama 'spects it on Saturday, then Harry can't pay your 'lowance. Jassy knows that now too."

"Okay, it means I have to clean my room when we get back to Miracle," Trina teased. "No wonder Jassy skipped church today."

Ann lowered her voice. "She wanted to wait until she had a chance to bring Reverend Tommy up to speed. She was worried there'd be too much drama from the Sweeney contingent and she's not going back to the homeplace until she has a guarantee she'll be treated right."

There were other times, other places, and other bases when he went to church, Derek thought. This happened to be one of the best. First, he had Kyra who knocked his proverbial socks off when she kissed him. Next, the sermon was a low-key, but powerful one. Third, he was with all sorts of friends in a town where he planned to find a home.

At the end of the service, he accompanied Kyra and the others to the Fellowship Hall to have doughnuts and coffee. Before she raced off to join the rest of the kiddoes, Devon reminded him to use his company manners and talk to all the people, not just the ones he knew, 'cause that was the best way to make friends. He promised to follow her directions.

Once they had their refreshments, Ann led the way to a long table with plenty of chairs, saying her parents would soon be along to join them. However, Ginger Madison was the only one who arrived, claiming her husband was tied up on what she referred to as some sort of association business.

"What's that?" Derek asked. "I didn't know there were any gangs in Baker City."

Ann laughed. "There aren't. Dad's the Prez for life of what's known as the BC Business Association. In other towns, it'd probably be the Chamber of Commerce. He keeps trying to get someone to take over for him, but nobody wants the job. What's up, Mother?"

"Nick MacGillicudy is attempting to talk your dad into opening an office here."

"Why would he need one?" Harry reached for the carafe at the end of the table and topped off their coffee cups. "Don't people have to come to your barns to see the horses?"

"It's not for us. It's for the Baker City Business Association. Nick thinks we should do an old-time Christmas event."

"What?" Ann wrinkled her nose. "It hasn't started snowing yet, but when it does, some of the roads near Baker City are impassable. We can't get in tourists."

"Oh, he doesn't want them. He wants a big shindig for everybody who lives in and near Baker City. He convinced Reverend Tommy to pull the Nativity scene out of storage. Nick promised to help refresh it. Don't be surprised when he suggests the kids at your school do a holiday pageant."

Ann tilted her head and glanced at Kyra. "I like it. Will you persuade Virginia Thompson to help? I'll line up the other teachers and we'll present it to the school board."

"Isn't Grandpa on that?" Trina asked. "He's liable to be

annoyed because you helped Jassy move off the Sweeney ranch and he'll need a new maid, cook and farmhand."

"Too bad, too sad." Ann tossed her head. "Unfortunately for him, we can outvote his misogynistic buns. Who is Dad planning to have run the new office?"

"That was something else Nick wanted. A job there," Ginger said. "He wants to be the new city manager. He explained to Frank that his father, Liam O'Leary, and some of Tex Hawke's other minions might go after members of a city council again if we held another election. However, Nick pointed out that they couldn't get rid of an employee hired by the Baker City Business Association since none of them are members. He says he isn't afraid of them, and he'll stick and stay."

"I thought he was a farrier," Ann said. "Granted, he's a crappy one. Dad told me what he did to my horse, Skyrocket, the last time he came to Majestyk Morgans while I was away. And Nick had already been told Sky was a rescue who'd suffered severe trauma."

"What did Nick do?" Kyra stiffened in the chair next to him.

"He ran a rope around his rear legs, threw him, belly-kicked him a few times, then hobbled him and trimmed his hooves. When he was turned loose, Skyrocket attacked Nick."

A tear streaked down Kyra's cheek. "I'm so sorry."

"For what?" Derek wrapped an arm around her shoulders. "It's not your fault. You have to let people own what they do. Sounds as if the guy's a real—" He stopped, putting two and two together. Nick must have been the guy she dated before him. What other reason would she have for taking responsibility for him?

"That's why Frank fired him, along with the groom who allowed Nick to bully the horse." Ginger sipped her coffee. "Granted, he'd already dumped a couple trainers and stomped one, putting the poor man in the hospital, but Frank insisted on finding someone else. He said he'd promised Ann before she went to Afghanistan that we'd take good care of her horse. I thought he should have put down the brute, but Frank was right. Cat O'Leary-McTavish managed to sort him out."

"She always had a way with horses even before she moved here and took on Baker City," Ann said. "You'll want her and Rob to walk through your new place, Waller."

"Why would she?" Derek asked.

"Because in Baker City, the ghosts are real." Kyra leaned against him for a moment. "You don't want to mess with them. It's why we depend on the O'Leary to handle them. Are you seriously considering moving here? I thought you were Army all the way."

"I was for thirty years." Derek stared into the lovely gray eyes. "It's long enough. I'm ready for a change."

"You'll have to tell me all about it."

"I will, but we'll do it later."

CHAPTER TEN

Moises always enjoyed Sunday services in Baker City. He especially liked listening to the choir who often featured teen singers. Reverend Tommy's sermons frequently reminded him of the preachers back home who exhorted the parishioners to do their best and be kind to each other. It amazed him to see Nick MacGillicudy in one of the pews today, but maybe he was on the road to redemption. The former madam had said she'd seen him in the café having breakfast and Nick not only paid for his meal, but he also left a tip. And he didn't let his little sister abscond with the money.

Zeke Garvey and Raven Driscoll-Barlow joined Moises when he followed the congregation into the Fellowship Hall for refreshments. Raven glanced around the room at the different family groups. "I don't see Jassy Sweeney anywhere. What's up with that? Usually, she helps her grandpa. Today he's with

Bendigo Hawke, some of the Hawke clan and only half of the Sweeney bunch."

"Scuttlebutt is she walked out Thanksgiving Day when he decided she should be replaced by a man on the Sweeney ranch." Zeke shook his head ruefully. "Someone should have taught him to respect women years ago."

"Well, when he joins us, we will." Raven smiled. "There's Sully and the Murphys. I'm going to visit my namesake and her twin sister. I'll catch up with you two at the café later."

"She has the right idea." Zeke gestured toward a large table on the far side of the room with a group, including a lovely dark-haired woman holding a little girl in a pink dress. They were surrounded by several boys, ranging in age from youngsters to teenagers. "Want to join us, Pride? The Garveys are always entertaining."

"Maybe later. For now, I'm going to check up on Nick and see what the man is doing to make amends." Moises frowned thoughtfully. "Our Christmas project isn't over yet."

"Nick has a long way to go before he becomes a real human being," Zeke agreed. "A few baby steps don't mean anything."

Church on Sunday was a must. Cat O'Leary-McTavish sat at one of the smaller tables in the corner, her husband, Rob, close by, holding their infant daughter. Their older girls were off visiting friends around the room and would return shortly with Devon Sweeney-Barrett since Penny Sinclair, their other best buddy was off to eastern Washington with her family for the holiday.

Cat smiled at Rob. They'd developed a strategy over the past year of using this social hour to let the residents of Baker City share their concerns. After they listened to the living ones, they'd go to the café and visit the cocktail lounge to deal with the ghosts who were even more talkative. She glanced at Nick MacGillicudy when he approached. It amazed her to see him here especially escorted by Frank Madison and Reverend Tommy. "What's going on?"

Frank spoke up first. "We want your help, Cat. It's time to open up an office for the Baker City Business Association and hire a city manager to deal with the day-to-day operations of the town. We plan to do it like the Vet Center. Nick talked to me about a job there."

"How is that?" Rob rocked the sleeping baby. "Are you planning to use one of the old houses you've bought over the years? You could have an office and visitor center in the front and living quarters in the rest of it."

"Exactly." Nick hesitated before gesturing to a chair. "Okay, if I sit down? I have other things I need to talk to you about."

Cat nodded, then looked at the older men. "All right. Do you want me to get Mayor O'Connell's approval? I don't think he'll mind. He wants to restore Baker City as much as we do. What else?"

"Nick's first project is to recreate the winter holiday festivals, so they're like what Baker City used to offer," Reverend Tommy said. "After that, he's going to find a way to finance a new town hall for meetings. There are several people like Debbie Ramsey and Summer O'Neill who won't attend church, so it's proven a little more difficult to get them involved in local activities."

"Nick's right about being the city manager," Frank added. "We can fire him if he doesn't do a good job, but it won't be like what happened ten years ago when Herman MacGillicudy and his friends went after our city council. By the time the furor died down, everyone had quit, including the current mayor."

"And when we tried to hold elections, there was more drama," Reverend Tommy added. "Nobody was willing to have their names on the ballots once Herman and his minions began harassing them. Frank's right about the Business Association hiring a manager. There probably won't be complaints about that, and we can ignore any that crop up, as long as Nick doesn't annoy the retailers who are actually paying his salary."

"I won't," Nick promised. "Since they'll have my back, I'll have theirs and I'll do what they want."

"That's right." Frank nodded. "The association already has lists of more endeavors for Nick to manage, things we haven't been able to do yet."

Cat watched the minister and the president of the business association walk away. Both men seemed excited about the new opportunities for their much-loved town. She eyed Nick. "Okay, what's on your mind? I don't know why you want to do this, considering the apple doesn't fall far from the proverbial tree and you have the rep of being a mean son-of-a—"

"I am, or rather I was, but I'm going to change. I swear it." Nick leaned forward. "You gotta make them stop."

"Make who stop? I didn't start anyone, so I have no idea what you're talking about. Your father?"

Nick shuddered. "No, when they go after him, everyone will

know. You're the O'Leary. Make 'em stop. Please. I've got it. I'll change. I went to Liberty Valley yesterday."

"Why?" Rob asked. "If you want something we don't have in Baker City, you can usually find it in Lake Maynard. Why drive all the way to Liberty Valley?"

"Because I wanted to sell my horseshoeing equipment and there's a school in Monroe that would buy my portable forge and the rest of my gear. I could sleep at a motel there. They don't have ghosts. I don't want to move to Liberty Valley."

"You don't have to move." When the baby woke and began to fuss, Cat reached for her. She took a moment to settle the infant against her chest. "I'm glad you've stopped shoeing, Nick, and it sounds like you have a good grasp on promotions that will help the town. I like the idea of an old-fashioned Christmas. My girls are already signed up for the Gingerbread House contest at the bakery."

"We'll do other fun events. Please make 'em stop."

"All right." Rob rested a hand on the other man's shoulder. "What did they do?"

"You believe me?" Nick heaved a sigh. "If anybody ever told me I'd be part of *A Christmas Carol*, I'd have said they were nuts. But I've seen the *Ghost of Christmas Past*. He was kind of a fun guy, and he showed me what this town could be like again. The *Ghost of Christmas Present* was rough and a little nasty about my family. Can't blame him after everything my father did to turn Baker City into dust. My dad is a major jerk, and I don't want to be one."

Cat snuggled the frazzled baby. In a few minutes, she'd have to discreetly arrange to nurse Claire, but that could wait until Nick left. "What about the *Ghost of Christmas Future*?"

"No, no, no!" Nick shook his head. "Marley was bad enough. Seeing him with half his head blown away totally freaked me out. I'll change. I don't want to see the next ghost. Make 'em stop. Please!"

"We can't promise anything," Rob said in even tones. "You've done a lot of bad things over the years, Nick, especially to those who couldn't defend themselves. You've hurt people too, like—"

"That's why I stopped doing horse biz. They're so big and they scare the hell out of me, but computers don't. And I've helped my sister, Dominique, when she's flipping houses. I'll do better."

"And you'll quit dating vulnerable women," Cat said. "Nobody should have their heart broken because you have all the depth of a cookie sheet. We're not plastic people, Nick. You have to stop acting like your father in every aspect of your life."

"I will." Nick froze in the chair. "Oh, my Gawd. You're talking about Kyra O'Neill, aren't you? She's told me more than once that she loves me, and I've treated her like—"

"Dirt," Rob agreed. "The ghosts don't appreciate that, and you grew up here. You should know how Baker City is by now. The haunts see it all and they express their opinions about it, even if most of their kin aren't sensitive enough to hear them, but you're related to the O'Learys. It's why you won't be able to ignore the spirits." He gestured toward the rest of the room. "Go try to make things right, Nick. We'll do our best with the spirits, but we're not promising anything."

"Okay, I appreciate you listening and agreeing to help me even though I've been a real asshat." Nick hurried away.

When he was out of earshot, Cat eyed her husband. "Sounds like a couple of the military ghosts have been having fun with him. I haven't heard a lot of civilians use the term, 'asshat' but it seems popular with prior service people."

Rob chuckled, then inclined his head in agreement. "You have a good point there, kitten. Let's chat about it with the vets when we hit the café later."

Kyra was on her second cup of coffee and contemplating another thickly frosted maple bar when Bendigo Hawke came across the room. After greeting all of them, he turned toward Trina. "Your grandpa wants you to come join the rest of the family."

"Sorry, I don't have "Welcome" tattooed on my forehead like Jassy and I'm not willing to pretend." Trina leaned back in her chair. "There's a reason I left home on my eighteenth birthday and moved in at Miracle Stable to work for Mindy. I'm never going back."

Obviously frustrated, Bendigo ran a hand through his black hair. "Look, I never asked your grandfather for your damned family property, and I don't want it."

"Sounds like you need to share that with Dwight Sweeney." Kyra flicked a glance at her roommate. "Trina, go tell the old cuss when it comes to choosing sides, you're on Jassy's. He should have learned women aren't second-class citizens a long time ago. Until he treats you and your sisters like all of you are as good as men, he has a problem."

"I can do that." Trina stood. "Any other words of advice?"

"Yeah, tell him the Hawkes have more money than lottery winners, so he should sell that hardscrabble, decrepit farmstead to Bendigo for a million bucks. Then, he could move to an old folks home, pay staff to take care of him for the rest of his life and he wouldn't need Jassy to come home and change his sheets when he wets the bed."

"Good points." Trina walked away to join her family at their table.

The comment earned shocked looks not only from Bendigo, but also from everyone else. Ginger Madison was the only one brave enough to ask the next question. "Kyra, are you serious?"

"Hell, yes! Over the past couple of years, I've heard all about Dwight's health issues. He calls different relatives and gets them to bring over candy or soda or pastries or cookies, things he shouldn't have. Jassy is the one who has to clean up after he loses control of his bladder or bowels when his blood sugar is out of whack."

"That's horrible." Ann took a deep breath. "Why hasn't she mentioned any of this to the family?"

Kyra laughed. "Oh, believe me, she has numerous times, but they don't listen because Dwight is so obnoxious. He gets really rude and calls her names when she tries to control his diet and keeps track of what kind of groceries come into the house. She also monitors his blood sugar, makes sure he gets his insulin and takes him to Doc on a regular basis."

"I didn't know he was diabetic," Bendigo said. "He was

griping at me because there wasn't any milk or ice-cream in the house, and I told him we'd swing by the mercantile on the way home."

"He was already lactose intolerant even before he got adult-onset diabetes." Kyra eyed Bendigo over the rim of her coffee cup. "Dairy makes his incontinence worse, so you'll have a hell of a mess to clean up if you buy that stuff. Jassy's not there to mop the floors or help him take a shower afterwards or do his laundry when he literally craps on himself or all over the house."

"She never said anything about that. He pitched a fit when she threw out the ice-cream, I brought him. I didn't know I was making things harder on her."

"She wouldn't tell you, Hawke," Ann said. "It'd embarrass her because he's her grandpa and she doesn't want anyone to pity him. I'll bet he's careful most of the time not to verbally abuse her and call her names when there's an audience. I've heard there's a link between diabetes and dementia in older people. He didn't hesitate to criticize her when Harry and I were there to get her things on Friday."

Harry nodded. "Now that you've had the sitrep, Hawke, if I were you, I'd talk to Doc MacGillicudy. Get a caregiver to come in and look after Dwight on a regular basis. Everybody knows the Hawkes have boatloads of bucks from their businesses in Texas."

"Be aware hiring help will irritate the other Sweeneys," Kyra added. "They have their minds set on Jassy picking up all the slack. It pissed me off when she'd visit us and cry while she told

Trina about the regular sabotage. Jassy is a real saint, but I'm not."

There was a long silence before Bendigo said, "Heather tells me that Linda MacGillicudy comes in to clean her place every week. Do you think she'd consider doing the Sweeney house too?"

"All you can do is ask." Ginger waved toward a table in the far corner. "Go check with her now. I always have her come around the holidays and deep clean my place before I start entertaining. Tell her that you expect to pay extra because she'll be dealing with medical waste."

"Thanks for the advice." Bendigo narrowed his cobalt-blue eyes. "I'll talk to Dwight about selling me the Sweeney place if nobody in his family wants it. The ground really isn't suitable for livestock or farming, even though Jassy manages to train horses there. The rugged terrain makes it a great place for me to train mercenaries, and we can't do that at the dude ranch."

After he strode away, Harry laughed. "Well, if that doesn't make the Sweeneys step up, I don't know what will. Turning their homeplace into a Nighthawke recruitment and training compound—"

"Yeah, that should be enough to shock them into next week," Derek agreed. "I had offers from them, Colter. What about you? Did you ever want to be an independent contractor?"

"Not my kind of circus and I'm not dealing with the kind of situations those guys and gals do." Harry shrugged. "I've done enough combat tours with the Army. When I retire, I'll join Uncle Dick and police Baker City."

Derek glanced at the slender blonde woman making the rounds. Dominique MacGillicudy was the perfect fashion plate in a light blue dress that clung to every curve and matched her eyes. When she spotted him, she hustled across the room. Matching stiletto heels made her taller than him.

Kyra nodded a greeting. "What's going on, Dominique?"

"I'm so glad you made it this weekend." Dominique focused on Derek and answered. "I have four new listings to show you. Two fixers and two turn-key possibilities. And I talked to the heirs of the former owner of the old auto repair shop. They're willing to entertain an offer. I have the keys so we can look at it."

"Sounds intriguing." Derek glanced at Kyra. "Got anything else to do now? Shall we go look at houses?"

That earned a steady look from Dominique. "Oh, I didn't realize you were a couple. My bad. Only one of them has a decent kitchen. We should start there."

"Or not." Looking nervous, Kyra hesitated, meeting Derek's gaze. "Are you sure about this? You just heard me being a real bitch to Bendigo Hawke."

Derek chuckled. "Honey, I've endured enough shitshows over the past thirty years to respect someone who calls it like she sees it."

"Kyra's known for doing that," Frank Madison commented. "We all respect her for it. Well, not Tex Hawke, but he's a quintessential politician who's already sold his soul and so have his minions."

"That's really true and my dad's one of them," Dominque agreed. "Now, let's go shopping."

Derek paused as Trina rejoined them. "How's your family?"

"Having tantrums all around because when Bendigo arrived after talking to you folks, he said he'd buy the Sweeney place from Grandpa, but he wasn't joining the family in the old school game of 'spinning the helmet' on Jacinth, whatever that means." Trina sat down between Ann and Ginger. "It sounded really bad."

"It is," Frank told her. "It's when soldiers ambush their commanding officer."

"Wow, that is bad." Trina topped off her cup with fresh coffee. "And it's not all. He said if it was part of the deal to get the property, then the Sweeneys needed to find another sucker. Oh, and he's researching appropriate foods for diabetics and if anybody brings over stuff Grandpa shouldn't have, it's going in the garbage. Grandpa started yelling at him and Bendigo said for him to 'man up' and take charge of his health so other people don't have to babysit him."

"I'm impressed." Derek rose to his feet. "Let's go look at property, Kyra. If you don't like the place, I'm not buying it. Well, except for the garage, of course. I need somewhere with a decent vehicle lift, jacks, presses, an engine hoist—"

"I'll take your word for it." Kyra laughed and stood. She fished her car keys out of her purse and passed them to Trina. "I'll see you back at the barn."

"Okay, but when you find the perfect house, I expect tours. And if you don't find it today, I get to go with you and Dominique next time."

"Works for me." Dominique started toward the door. "You can always come with us when we take Cat O'Leary-McTavish through a prospective home. I'm beginning to learn most of my clients in Baker City want her approval."

"Only the smart ones." Derek took Kyra's hand and they headed for the door. "Talk to me. What does your dream house have?"

CHAPTER ELEVEN

Hand in hand with Derek, Kyra headed toward the door, listening to Dominique's chatter about the various properties. Halfway there, she saw Nick. The big, blond guy started in their direction, then stopped. He waved at her, and she nodded at him. He might not realize it yet, but they were through, and she was good with that.

In the parking lot, Dominique led the way to her car, a fairly new four-wheel-drive Jeep. She unlocked it and removed her laptop. "Okay, let's preview these places and rule out anything that won't work. No point in wasting our time." She clicked the mouse and proceeded to pull up views of a series of reasonably priced bungalow-style homes. "These are three or four-bedroom houses, all with two or more bathrooms. Which one would you like to see first?"

"None of the above." Grimacing, Kyra wrinkled her nose.

"They look like cookie-cutter clones. Don't you have anything with some soul? And I'm not talking about ghosts."

Dominique giggled. "Okay, just remember you asked for it. What about this one? It's walking distance from the garage. It needs work, but it's had some updates already."

"I'll take your word for it." Derek studied the picture of the two-story Victorian style home with decorative gingerbread trim along the eaves and a tower on the far-left corner. The pale green exterior definitely needed repainting. More of the white trim around the wrap-around porch required repairs. "Are you sure you want to see it, Kyra? It looks like trouble to me."

She smiled at him. "The good thing about a fixer-upper is we can 'lowball' the owners because of all the work it will take to restore its character and charm. Let's go check out its potential."

"You've got it," Derek said.

It didn't take long to reach the house in the middle of a half-acre lot. They walked up the driveway and Kyra saw a detached two-car garage with a new metal roof off to the right. She liked the large, fenced yard on the corner lot. "There's plenty of space for additional parking or even a garden."

"Flowers or vegetable?" Derek asked.

"Why not both?" Dominique gestured to the side yard and three apple trees still laden with fruit. "You could always add more and have a real orchard."

"Not a bad idea." Kyra agreed.

Dominique gingerly led the way up a cracked cement walkway to the porch. "Watch your step. I told the owners to fix the deck, but they haven't yet. There are several rotten spots."

"Another price drop," Kyra said cheerfully and squeezed Derek's hand. "This is so fun."

"Glad you think so. Why do I believe there will be a major 'honey-do' list in my future?"

Both women laughed and Dominique unlocked the key-box attached to the front door. "Okay, here we go!"

They immediately entered a living room with bright pumpkin paint on the walls. An arched doorway led to the dining-room. Another opened onto the kitchen. It had hardwood countertops, vintage cedar cabinets, a farmhouse sink, and a butler's pantry. When they walked through the old-fashioned mudroom with room for a washer and dryer, Kyra spotted the back door. Dominique warned them not to try using it because she didn't think a broken hinge had been repaired, but said the driveway circled around, which would make it convenient for bringing in groceries.

The rest of the main level included an office with French doors and two bay windows, and the master bedroom had three huge closets, but no en-suite. There was only one bathroom for the entire lower level. While it didn't have a tub, it did have a shower. The two spacious bedrooms upstairs each had large closets. The upper level had a full bathroom, but the owners had started renovations and hadn't finished them. The second-story, tower room had been turned into a quintessential man-cave complete with a bar and a pool table.

Derek chuckled and wrapped an arm around Kyra's waist. "I know what you're going to say. Another price drop, right?"

"Right!" She frowned thoughtfully. "I think there might be enough space to modify the downstairs bathroom for guests and turn one of the closets into an en-suite. Dominique, do you have a tape measure?"

"Yes, and an idea." Frowning thoughtfully, Dominique held up her hand. "What if you contacted Hawke Construction to give you a bid on the remodeling? We could use that for leverage if you decide to make an offer."

"Sounds like a winner." Kyra pulled out her phone. "We also need to call Cat O'Leary-McTavish and see when she can visit. Who are the sellers?"

Dominique winced. "Don't hate me. It belongs to your cousins. They bought it as an investment and then barely did squat with it because it was too much like work. They claimed they couldn't. The house was haunted because tools were moved, lights and music went on and off, objects were thrown at them, doors and windows slammed—you know—the usual drill in Baker City when the ghosts are annoyed."

"Now, I definitely want it," Kyra said. "It will be so much fun to fix it up and rub my family's noses in it when we invite them to the housewarming." She tilted her head to one side. "Are you scared yet, Waller? I warned you at church. I am a real bitch, and I don't say it like it's a bad thing. As for the haunts, when and if we get the place, Cat can tell them to cut the crap. They're not running us out."

He tipped up her chin and brushed her lips with his. "And I already told you, Kyra O'Neill. Growing up in the Army means I want someone strong enough to watch my six."

Kyra sighed. "I've been around Debbie Ramsey long enough to know what that means. I'll cover your back as long as you cover mine."

"Oh, such a winner." Dominique beamed at the two of them. "It's so good to see you with a real man, Kyra. I love it. Okay, we're going to do some research before Derek makes an offer. We're keeping Kyra's name out of it for now, so the O'Neill bunch doesn't jack up the price."

Frank Madison and his wife had taken Nick to inspect three of the houses on the main street in Baker City. Frank admitted they'd purchased the older homes to keep Herman MacGillicudy from tearing down the structures. They chose one across from the hardware store for the new Baker City Business Association office. Frank said he'd contact a sign painting company and Nick suggested they talk to his sister, Dominique.

"Why would we do that?" Ginger tucked her hands into her coat pockets. "We're not selling the place. We don't need a real estate broker."

"She did the new signs for Hawke's Horse Heaven and the Cedar Creek Guest Ranch. She loves to paint. She hoped to be an artist." Nick stared at the clouds forming on the horizon. If the temperature continued to drop, they'd have snow before long. "Reed College in Portland, Oregon accepted her in their art program. So did a few other colleges in California, but my mom couldn't afford it and my dad —."

Ginger nodded. "We'll call her about a sign. It's never too late to follow a dream, Nick. You might suggest she apply to the colleges again."

"No, she has another dream now. She's saving Baker City

from my old man. She told me she's making sure he doesn't get any of the properties here. It really pisses him off when she gets another one listed on the state historical register. I don't know if you've noticed or not, but the school, church, café, and mercantile already have their plaques. The feedstore should have one next year."

Frank passed a set of keys to Nick. "That's awesome. Your cousin, Linda, said she'd have her crew clean the place so it will be ready for your furniture today. Jack is rounding up a crew of his friends to help move the heavy stuff. He'll meet you at your trailer in a half hour. Let us know if you need anything else."

"We told Maxine to let you have credit at the mercantile for the next two weeks until you have your first paycheck, and then we'll renegotiate the amount," Ginger said. "It's the same thing we do for the teachers. Food only. No alcohol or tobacco."

"Thank you." Nick shook hands with the older couple before he headed toward his pickup. He hadn't expected the kindness they'd shown him or the willingness to accept his ideas, especially the job as city manager. Of course, it helped to have Reverend Tommy, Cat O'Leary-McTavish, and her husband on his side. *I'm not screwing up this time. Not ever again!*

Members of the congregation had slowly slipped out of the Fellowship Hall, a few at a time. Cat O'Leary-McTavish wasn't quite ready to leave yet. She'd wait until she was sure nobody else wanted to talk to her. She'd watched the silver-haired patriarch of the Sweeney clan stomp out of the room, banging his walker on the tile floor. Dwight had yelled at his grown children, pitching the kind of tantrum that would have sent her daughters to what Cat thought of as 'Time-Out City' at the kitchen table.

The twins hated the punishment, which was the purpose of it. She made them sit in utter silence for nine minutes, one minute for each year, and contemplate their sins. When she first moved to the dude ranch, Rob had still been in his ghostly mode, determined to haunt her. After dealing with several of his spooky antics, the culmination had been when he played games with the lights, turning them on and off while she attempted to prepare supper. It'd shocked the girls when she'd sent him to his room for two hours. Of course, Cat thought she was dealing with an imaginary friend.

Turnabout was fair play, she thought, eyeing the ruggedly handsome man across the table from her. It'd shocked her to discover he was real and now they were parents again. Cat opened her blouse, arranging it and her bra so Claire could nurse, gasping when the hungry baby latched onto her nipple. She arranged the shawl over her shoulders to be discreet. "I'll bet Moises Pride played Marley. He's the only one I know who died by gunshot."

"Are you going to call him out for breaking the rule of nothing bloody or gory?"

"No. He didn't do it to a child, or an innocent, and I don't recall telling him not to show his death to a selfish adult." Cat began to smile and then to giggle. "I've got to admit I'd have loved to see our town's ghostly version of *A Christmas Carol*."

"Well, they certainly scared Nick onto the straight and

narrow. Are you going to stop the visit of the *Ghost of Christmas Future*?"

Cat stroked Claire's soft cheek while she nursed. "Not unless Skyrocket and a dozen other horses practice forgiveness and agree whoever it is shouldn't pay a call tonight."

"You know they won't."

"I know and neither will I." Cat paused. "I wonder if they'll let me give them a list of people to reform for the next ten years. Maybe we could start with Dwight Sweeney."

"And build up to Herman MacGillicudy and your father."

"Oh, and Tex Hawke and his minions," Cat said.

Rob chuckled. "And we've barely started."

Sunday afternoons, the ghosts always filled the cocktail lounge long before living customers arrived. Moises circulated among them, feeling welcome as he chatted to many of his new friends. Ling Zhao and her husband paused to talk to him, and he promised once again that she'd have her opportunity to visit Nick soon.

Several of the ghosts had seen him eating breakfast at the café before he went to the church. He'd done some sort of business with the minister and the head of the business council, but Moises had also seen him talking to the medium and her husband. Had he ratted them out? Nobody seemed to know yet.

A hush fell as Cat O'Leary-McTavish entered the room, baby Claire in her arms and Rob Hendrickson behind them. Cat glanced around. "Okay, folks. I've been hearing all about your holiday hijinks. Whose bright idea was this?"

"Ours," Zeke Garvey and Raven Driscoll-Barlow immediately said, their voices chiming together. "It was something to do to bring Christmas to Baker City."

"Do we have to stop?" Mayor O'Connell asked. "Everyone's enjoying it and we're all helping."

"Oh no." Cat held up her hand. "You don't get to stop. You have to keep going and next time, Rob and I want to help. Santa's busy right now, so we're making a list of who's been naughty and who needs a ghostly intervention."

"Or even a ghastly one." Rob looked around the room. "But no blood, guts, or gore where the kids, tweens and teens are concerned. That particular rule created by the first O'Leary still applies."

Moises drifted in their direction, waiting until the rest of his ghostly companions had moved away. He met Cat's eyes. "It was me. I'm the one who really started it. Master Sergeant Garvey and Top-First Sergeant Barlow just want to protect me."

"Of course, they do. It's their job to look out for the enlisted," Rob said. "It's fine, Pride."

"But what do you want for Christmas, Moises?" Cat asked. "What can we give you?"

"I got it. I'm home and I have it." Moises glanced over his shoulder at the other ghosts. "May I still send out the *Ghost of Christmas Future*? She's so excited about visiting Nick MacGillicudy tonight."

"On one condition." Cat smiled, mischief lighting her green eyes. "We want to see her in all her ghostly glory."

"Then she can rock and roll," Rob added. "Merry Ghostmas to one and all!"

Usually, he met his friends at the cocktail lounge at Pop's café or else at one of the bars in Lake Maynard. They hung out, drank together, and played pool if there wasn't live music. Yes, Frank Madison had said his son, Jack would be over to help pack up the trailer, but Nick hadn't been a hundred-percent sure that would happen. To his amazement, it did. Jack arrived with his former brother-in-law, Will Sweeney, and some of the other guys.

While Jack helped Nick break down the king-size bed, Will went to the kitchen and wrapped the dishes in newspaper. Two of their friends started work in the living-room and a third hit the bathroom. "Can't believe we're knocking this out so fast," Nick said. "I appreciate it, Jack."

"No worries." In a flannel shirt, hacked-off, ankle-length jeans and thick wool socks, Jack Madison was tall and muscled from years of logging. He had his mother's gold hair and his father's spring green eyes. "Thanks for not kicking Will to the moon. The guy's trying to suck up to us because he wanted to spend time with my niece, Devon, this weekend, and she wasn't having it."

"She's a kid. Why does she get to make that decision?"

"Lots of drama while Ann was away on that last combat tour." Jack shrugged. "My older half-sisters are real witches. When Will dumped Devon on them, it wasn't good for the kid.

Plus, he took her cat to the pound. By the time my folks found out about that stunt, it'd already been adopted by someone else. So, when he offered to take her to see Santa, Devon refused. Said he probably didn't mean it and she'd go with my mom or her stepdad, who never lies."

Nick froze. "Wow. Was Will lying to her?"

"Who knows? Like Devon says, he's done it lots of times. The kid can be a real brat, but what kind of jerk deliberately tries to hurt a little girl's feelings?" Jack carried the footboard to the bedroom door. "My mom and Devon plan to do a lot of Christmas shopping so she'll get to see Santa and his helpers plenty of times. Dad said you were going to organize some holiday events in Baker City. Are you hiring someone to play Santa?"

"Definitely. I'm going to talk to Summer O'Neill and see if he and Mrs. Claus can hang out at the feedstore because that's where the sleigh already is waiting. Haven't quite decided how to fake some reindeer, but I'll figure out a way."

"Brilliant!" Jack high-fived him. "I think you've already found your niche, my man."

"I hope you're right." Nick nearly said he admired the other man's niece. Imagine being able to figure out her father was a heartbreaker when she was only seven. *Good heavenly days! I'm damn near thirty years older and it took a ghost to tell me my dad is an utter asshat and got his kicks trying to destroy people.*

Two hours later, the guys had left with their fully loaded pickup trucks. Nick locked up the trailer and headed for his own rig. A late-model, white Cadillac pulled into the driveway. A stocky man in a three-piece suit with neatly trimmed silver blond hair came toward Nick and he reached in his jeans for the keys to the trailer. "Hey, Dad. Glad you're here."

"What?" Shock spread across Herman MacGillicudy's ruddy features. "That's the last thing I expected you to say. What are you doing?"

"Moving on." Nick handed him the ring of keys. "I have a new job and it includes a decent place to live. Here you go."

"You're a horseshoer."

"Not anymore. Never liked the job. Never wanted it." Nick met his father's gaze. "I did it to please you, but I'm thirty-six years old. I'm giving that up too."

Herman blinked. "I don't understand."

"I quit. It's stupid of me to try and make you happy. I'm not the son you want. I never was." Nick opened the driver's door. "Go have a good life, Dad. Maybe, along the way, you'll figure out what you want besides destroying Baker City and wrecking lives. I'm not following in your footsteps any longer. I want people to love me, not fear me."

CHAPTER TWELVE

He enjoyed spending most of Thanksgiving weekend in Baker City with his ghostly friends while they did their reenactment of *A Christmas Carol*. Everything was going well, so Moises decided to pop into Miracle Riding Stable on Sunday night. Granted, Debbie Ramsey's family wasn't due back until the next day, but it was the perfect time to check on all the critters. The dogs, cats and horses were undoubtedly missing him as much as he missed them.

When he arrived, he floated through the house. The two cats curled up in one of the living-room recliners listening to the stereo tuned to a local radio station playing one holiday song after another. Moises hummed along while he went in search of the dogs. He found them visiting with Trina Sweeney and Kyra O'Neill while they mucked stalls. The young cattle dog raced to greet him, winding around his insubstantial legs, and the collie-mix growled at him.

"Oh, come on. You know me by now." Moises glanced past her and saw Derek Waller helping with horse care. "Well, this is working out just like I hoped."

He drifted closer and heard the three of them discussing their plans for the next day. Trina planned to go shopping with her sister, while Kyra and Derek intended to preview a house with the manager of Hawke Construction. In the afternoon, Cat O'Leary-McTavish would inspect not only it, but also the auto-repair garage Derek wanted to buy. If there weren't any unseen guests, he and Dominique MacGillicudy would write up offers on both places.

"I can help with that," Moises told them, although he knew none of the three could hear him. "I'll go back to the cocktail lounge and get the mayor involved. We want this to work out for the two of you. You deserve to be happy."

After the tour of the house in Baker City that afternoon, Dominique took them to see the one-time, auto repair place. Derek inspected the equipment but claimed to be unimpressed by the various messes left behind by the original owner. He'd supervised enough motor pools over the years that he wanted everything to have its place and to be in that place. It was safer than seeing tools scattered on the floor rather than hanging on the walls. Even the office was a disaster. Rats had chewed through the papers on the desk and made nests in the filing cabinets.

Dominique explained the old man actually didn't retire. He

died and his heirs were too busy squabbling over their inheritance to continue the business or make it a showplace, which would increase the potential price. Kyra told him to 'lowball' the grown kids. He could bring in his buddies to help clean and organize the shop before he reopened it. Plus, they'd have Cat O'Leary-McTavish and her husband walk through the place and obtain the owner's blessing.

Short on time, they opted for lunch at the café, then picked up a frozen pizza and a sixpack of beer at the mercantile. Kyra expected him to drop her at the stable for chores, but he volunteered to stay and shovel horsy poop with her and Trina. Normally, Jason would have been here too, but he'd been co-opted by his family to visit relatives.

When they finished taking care of the horses, Trina said it was her turn to claim the shower and change clothes. She'd spend the night with her sister so they could make an early start and hit several holiday doorbuster sales first thing Monday morning. Sure, that was the story, but it wasn't the entire truth and Kyra knew it.

Granted, the barn manager apartment had two bedrooms, in addition to the shared bathroom, living-room and eat-in kitchen. It still wasn't that large. It meant having male company could be embarrassing, so they'd reached an agreement. Whichever one of them was solo that night would sleep elsewhere unless the other said she'd go home with the guy.

If she stayed over with Nick, Kyra often found herself cleaning up his trailer the next day because she couldn't stand looking at a human pigsty. Thankfully, she no longer had that mucking to do. It was another good point about ending things with him. Her gaze lingered on Derek. He was such a hunk in his dark sweater and stonewashed jeans. Once again, she found herself admiring his rugged features. No wonder she actually liked him. She'd spent more hours with Derek Waller in the last four and a half days than she had in five years with Nick.

Once Trina left, Derek went with Kyra to take home the dogs. They fed them and the cats, then returned to the apartment. While they shared a pizza and drank beer, they discussed paint colors for the house in Baker City. Derek vetoed the cream or eggshell that Kyra suggested for the living room, saying it'd be too stark.

After thirty years in the Army, he had enough of regulation white walls and other required pastel colors. She hadn't known he planned to move here, and that was a pleasant surprise. How could she learn everything about him in one weekend? It was impossible. *More to come,* she thought. *But nothing I can't deal with!*

"Don't tell me you want to keep that bright pumpkin color in the living-room." Kyra shuddered at the idea. "Why not use it for an accent? The other walls could be a lighter shade of orange."

"Sounds like we might need to visit the hardware store in Baker City tomorrow and see what paint options Aiden O'Leary has to offer." Derek picked up another slice of pizza. "Guess I better head for the hills or Colter's place before it gets much later."

"Or I could open a bottle of wine and we'll argue about what we're doing with the kitchen."

"If we did, I wouldn't be driving—" He paused. "I'd have to sack out on your couch."

She finished off her beer and eyed him before shaking her head. "It's not big enough for the two of us."

A long silence and then he asked cautiously. "Are you propositioning me?"

"If you have to ask, I must not be doing it right."

He stood, drank the remainder of his beer, and put the can in the recycle bin. "You're doing just fine, honey. Let's go."

She rose to her feet and snagged his calloused hand, drawing him in the direction of her bedroom. "This way, Derek."

"Okay but remember to tell me what you like so I don't screw it up."

She stopped in the hallway long enough to kiss him, a quick light tease of their lips. "No worries. If you haven't realized it yet, I'm very bossy."

"That definitely works for me." His mouth captured hers.

His sister, Dominique, showed up after most of the furniture had been placed in the appropriate rooms. She made the bed and stuck around to help hang curtains. She walked through the old two-story house with Nick. "So, what's the plan for the living-room? Why isn't your TV on the wall yet?"

"This is going to be the new Baker City Business Association office." Nick gestured to the desk in the front corner and the large table in the middle of the room, surrounded by an assortment of their grandmother's mismatched, antique chairs. "We'll be holding some of the meetings here, not just at Pop's Café. Frank Madison will be getting in touch with you about painting a new sign. I was bragging about the ones you've done for the dude ranch and Durango Hawke."

"And you're staying here because—"

"I'm the new city manager. First things first, I'll be facilitating the town celebration of Christmas. Any ideas where we can have a tree lighting ceremony?"

"Sure." Dominique led the way through the kitchen to the back door. She ushered him to the wrap-around porch. She pointed down the street to a view of the long-abandoned park and playfield dimly lit by the vintage lampposts. "Look at that giant cedar in the middle. It's perfect. All you have to do is round up people to help mow the grass, take out the blackberries and other weeds and clean up the garbage. Frank Madison might be able to hire one of the logging companies because some of them aren't in the woods right now and the employees are on standby. They'll be drawing their unemployment soon. There's even electricity in the old gazebo. Want me to organize ornaments and lights for the tree?"

"Definitely."

"Okay and you talk to Rick O'Connell about getting the fire department to use one of their trucks to put the star at the top. You're going to have so much fun, Nicky. I'm glad you're doing something you want to do. You'll be so good at it." Dominique hesitated. "What about Daddy? Does he know about your new job?"

"I told him when I returned the keys to his trailer." Nick shrugged. "And then I said I wasn't living the rest of my life in his shadow. That's over, Dom."

"I'm glad, big bro." Dominique repeated and hugged him.

"Now, come on. I'm going to help you finish settling into this place and then I'll buy you dinner at the café.

She was true to her word. When he returned after supper, he walked through the house. The large living-room was ready for business. He closed the drapes, grateful Linda MacGillicudy washed the windows when she was here earlier in the day. She'd mopped the floors and vacuumed the carpets. She'd scrubbed both bathrooms. The one downstairs would be for visitors, and he'd use the upstairs one near the master bedroom. He'd use the other two bedrooms as a sitting area and a den.

All of the day's activities overwhelmed him, and he decided to call it a night. He switched off the lights and headed for the staircase. Halfway up, he froze. Someone in a long, dark coat stood waiting on the landing. Nick realized he could see through his guest, a petite Asian woman. "Oh no. Not again. I talked to Cat O'Leary-McTavish. She said she'd tell you I was done."

"We're not." The woman said. "You started a new path."

"I've changed," Nick agreed. "So, you can go now."

She laughed, a sweet but deadly sound. "Not without you. Come along. We're seeing what happens if you stray."

"I don't want to see that future."

"Too bad. We'll go now." She gestured and he discovered they were outside.

Snow crunched under his feet. He stumbled and caught himself. Ashes and burned-out buildings lined the main street. A sign swung in the night air near a blackened beam. "Pop's Café."

"What happened?" Nick demanded. "Where is everybody?"

"Your father and his friends managed to buy everything after an arsonist set Baker City ablaze during the wildfire season." The ghost kept walking and pointed toward where the church once stood. Now, it was a gaping hole, another scorched skeleton of a structure with only the remnants of the bell tower still visible. "They left the graveyard."

"I don't want to go there."

"It's where all your relatives are now." She turned away. "Come along. We'll visit later. Let's go see what Herman's made of the place."

Nick shuddered, hearing the roar of machinery. He already knew. Bulldozers, front-end loaders, and trucks ran at the far end of the street. As they approached, he saw a huge gravel pit. It wasn't a surprise.

He'd heard his father discuss the process of obtaining rock before. Miners had torn away the layers of dirt, using large stripping machines. Once the rock and gravel below the surface could be seen, the material was easily extracted using front-end loaders and other large machines. Then, the gravel was washed, sorted, and prepared for shipping to plants or other manufacturing facilities.

Horror-stricken, he glanced behind him and realized the hotel his sister wanted to restore was one of the casualties. He stared at the desolate remains of his home-town. "Is this what will happen if I fail to stand up to him and his minions?"

"One man can make a difference," she said. "You've started. Now, we go to the cemetery."

"I don't want to see that. You already said my relatives are there. What about my sisters?"

"One died in the fire that took her realty. The other is in a coma in a Liberty Valley hospital."

Nick shuddered. "No. Can't we see something better? What will happen if I keep standing up, doing the right thing?"

"All right." She waved her hand. The pit vanished.

This time when he looked down the street, he heard music and saw brilliant multi-colored lights on the familiar buildings. In the refurbished city park, he spotted the giant evergreen decorated for the holiday. Snow covered the streets, roofs, and sidewalks. Lights shone through the windows of the old MacGillicudy hotel, and there were cars parked in front of the restored business. He recognized Twila Garvey surrounded by her boys, holding her daughter's hand as they headed up the walk. He followed the other guests, pausing when he saw his pickup parked close by.

As he watched, a stranger opened the passenger door. A woman. She turned and spoke to the driver. In a few moments, he followed her, carrying a blonde toddler in a red velvet dress. "Come on, princess. Let's go see Santa."

"That's me," Nick whispered.

"It's a possibility," the woman agreed. "Another one is the grave in the cemetery next to your sister's."

"No. This is the one I want, not that."

"Remember your decision and don't make me visit you again."

"Okay. You've got a deal."

They made love three times that night. Granted, the first time was a bit different—maybe awkward—was a better choice of words, Derek thought, but he'd ensured she was satisfied before he finished. The second bout was even better and the third rocked her world and his. In the morning, he followed her into the bathroom. Sex in the shower was a great way to start their day. Afterwards, they had breakfast together and then he helped her in the barns before he left.

She'd agreed to meet him in town for the walk-throughs of the house and garage with the foreman of Hawke Construction and the medium. If everything passed muster, they'd return to the realtor's office to write up the two offers. When he arrived at Colter's place, he found Harry in the kitchen. Ann and Devon had already left for school. The little girl's half-grown, collie-mix pup slept in his cave under the table.

Harry poured coffee into two mugs and passed one to Derek. "Ann said you were looking at the garage yesterday. What did you think of it?"

"It's do-able. I'll need help to clean it up and get ready for business. Are you in?"

"Of course. Just let me know when. I know a few kids in the battalion who always want extra bucks, and they'll jump in when I call." Harry leaned against the counter. "Is this when I ask why you missed curfew last night, Waller?"

Derek grinned. "Shove it, Colter. What's on the agenda today since we're not due back at work until tomorrow? I don't have to be in town until noon when I meet Kyra, the manager from Hawke Construction, Cat O'Leary-McTavish, and Dominique MacGillicudy at the house. Want to join us?"

"You bet." Harry drank more coffee. "It's going to be good having a decent mechanic in Baker City. I'm not the only one saying it. You may not get Sullivan Murphy's or Rob Hendrickson's classic Mustangs, but the rest of us will like having you here and not being forced to take our rigs to Lake Maynard."

"Oh, I'll get the Mustangs sooner or later," Derek said. "I can't pass up the opportunity to fuss over them. When their owners learn I won't hurt their four-wheel babies, they'll share them."

Moises Pride arrived at the Victorian house shortly before Kyra and Derek did with their entourage. He waited on the porch until the front door opened and a short, plump, silver-haired woman in a flowered housedress—another ghost—invited him inside. "I'm Nora Garvey. How can I help you?"

"I'm Moises Pride. I'm new in town and the mayor put me in charge of reforming Nick MacGillicudy with our *Christmas Carol* project."

"Doesn't that sound like fun?" Nora gestured for him to follow her inside. The door closed behind them. "Come meet my husband and tell us what we can do."

"Well, the project is wrapping up," Moises admitted. "But I was also getting Kyra O'Neill together with a former soldier who wants to re-open the auto repair place, so folks here won't have to take their cars to Lake Maynard."

"Oh, that's a good idea." Nora ushered him into the living room where her husband, an insubstantial ghost in rough, work clothes sat in a rocking chair watching a John Wayne movie on the large flat screen TV. "This is Moises Pride, dear. Moises, my husband, Seamus Garvey."

"Are you related to Zeke Garvey?" Moises asked. "He's been teaching me how things work in Baker City and what I can do now that I'm dead."

Seamus nodded. "He's my brother's grandson. We'll have to stop by Pop's one of these nights and visit him. We've been rather busy here, keeping out the low-lifes."

"I wanted to talk to you about that." Moises brought the older couple up to speed on the potential sale to Derek Waller who was moving to town and needed a place to live. "With any luck at all, he'll marry Kyra O'Neill—"

"And they want to live here?" Nora settled into the adjacent rocker and picked up her knitting. "We want a decent family in our home. We lived here, raised our children, spoiled their kids and then those O'Neills came and painted the place in such garish colors." She pointed to the bright orange walls and the brilliant white archway into the dining room. "So very vulgar."

"What they did to my study was disgusting." Seamus stood and drifted toward the tower room. "I found the knotty-pine paneling years ago and installed it myself. Come look at what they did."

Moises floated after the elderly ghost. The two of them stopped in the doorway and he saw a huge screen on the wall and fancy chairs. "Is it supposed to be a home theater?"

"Yes. As if this wasn't bad enough, they destroyed Nora's sewing room upstairs. They took away all her quilting things, including the frame I built for her and made it into a disgusting man-cave. We couldn't allow it to continue. We drove them away."

"I don't blame you." Moises heard a key in the front door lock and turned to see Dominique MacGillicudy enter the house accompanied by Jeff Ransom, a tall, brown-haired man who wore a dark three-piece suit, a white shirt, black tie, and highly polished dress shoes. In his right hand, he held a thickly carved wooden cane. Derek and Kyra were behind her, and Cat O'Leary-McTavish and her husband followed the couple.

Cat paused when she saw them. "Hello, Moises. Introduce me to your friends, please."

Moises obeyed the medium's directions. "Cat, this is Seamus Garvey. He and his wife, Nora, lived here a very long time. Seamus, this is Cat O'Leary-McTavish and her husband, Rob Hendrickson, who always help us out with our ghostly problems."

Kyra gasped. "Seamus Garvey? I can't believe it. This is such an honor. We studied your opinions so much in law school."

"His opinions?" Cat repeated. "I don't understand."

"Case law," Kyra explained. "Seamus Garvey is or rather was a judge in Lake Maynard. All of his decisions were upheld by the Washington Supreme Court in Olympia, which is very rare. He's brilliant."

"Oh, I wouldn't go that far." Still, Seamus looked very pleased by the praise. "And as for you, young lady. What kind of lawyer are you? Criminal or civil?"

Rob passed on the questions and Kyra explained she no longer practiced law. She taught horseback riding at Miracle Stable outside of town. The comment drew Jeff Ransom's attention. "My sister-in-law, Heather, says you should consider opening a small office here to help women with their legal issues. She has problems with George O'Connell and the way he handled her inheritance from her grandparents. Even though he knew she was in Tennessee, he didn't look for her there."

"Finding missing heirs is difficult and George is a decent attorney," Kyra said. "He represented Amarillo Hawke, your wife, in her emancipation case when she was barely sixteen and won. He outmaneuvered me. I quit working for her father shortly afterwards."

That earned her a long look not only from Jeff, but also from Seamus Garvey. Derek wrapped his hand around hers. "How did George do that?"

Kyra shrugged. "I had to send documents to him and the family willing to take in Amarillo and her baby. The Petrocelli's own a half-dozen restaurants in the local area, and they had several lawyers who helped George."

"And you lost against an entire team of legal eagles?" Derek drew her closer. "No shame there, honey. You were out-gunned. You didn't need to resign."

"Sure, she did." Jeff limped into the one-time den. "Tex Hawke and his minions don't handle defeat well. Better to walk away alive and stay that way than deal with an upset politician who thinks he's omnipotent. Now, come talk to me, Kyra, and bring along the judge and Cat. What do you two want me to do with this monstrosity? After, we decide that we'll figure out what's next."

CHAPTER THIRTEEN

Humming a new Baker City version of an old holiday fave, Moises floated into the cocktail lounge at Pop's Café. "We wish you a Merry Ghostmas. We wish you a Merry Ghostmas. Wish you a Merry Ghostmas and a haunted New Year—"

"I don't think it's how the song goes, Pride," Zeke Garvey announced from his favorite table in the center of the room. "What have you been doing?"

"Visiting your family. I didn't know you were related to a famous judge, Seamus Garvey."

"I haven't thought about them in years since they passed away ages ago," Zeke admitted. "Are they still here in Baker City?"

"Haunting their house." Moises sat down across from him. "Did you know your Grandaunt Nora won all sorts of prizes for her quilts?"

"Actually, I did. We, Twila, and I received one of them as a wedding present." Zeke smiled at the memory. "Grandaunt Nora explained the *Double Wedding Ring* quilt pattern is a traditional symbol of love and romance with its interlocking rings symbolizing marriage. Twila cherished it and she still has it on our bed. I guess I should say, 'her' bed, but it doesn't feel that way yet."

Raven Driscoll-Barlow joined them. She must have heard his comment because she added. "Doesn't feel that way to me either when I visit my husband. What's happening, Pride? How's your matchmaking?"

"It's good. Kyra and Derek visited Seamus and Nora Garvey's house and all of them are in accord. Hawke Construction will finish the renovations. When we visited the auto-shop, the original owner, Lorcan O'Leary, was there. He's thrilled an army vet wants to take over the place and apologized for not G.I.'ing things before he died."

"Did he have any warning?" Raven asked. "Or was it a surprise to him like it was to me?"

"A heart attack while he was doing an oil change three years ago," Moises said. "When he heard Sergeant-Major Waller plans to hire a crew of US Army vets to help clean and organize, Lorcan couldn't be happier. Turns out he did his twenty. Served in Korea, then in Vietnam with Rob Hendrickson. It was old-home week."

Raven gaped at Moises. "Rob Hendrickson, the O'Leary's husband? I don't understand. He's alive and he's barely thirty-something. How could he serve in a war fifty-plus years ago?"

"I'm not sure how he changed things, but Cat O'Leary-McTavish told me he was a ghost at the dude ranch when she moved here." Moises spotted the mayor arriving. "I bet he knows. We can ask him."

"Believe me, we will," Zeke said. "If there's a way to return home to Twila, I want it."

"Me too," Raven agreed. "Not to your wife but to my husband, Kord."

Accompanied by his long-time crony, Newt O'Leary, Mayor O'Connell glided toward them. "Have you seen Nick MacGillicudy at work, Pride? The man already has one of the logging companies cleaning up the old town park to have a tree-lighting ceremony next weekend. Meantime, Nick's helping Reverend Tommy set up a nativity scene at the church. He's truly reformed."

"Ling Zhao told me that last night when she finished her stint as the *Ghost of Christmas Future*," Moises concurred. "She reminded Nick if he stayed on the path he'd started, she wouldn't visit him again. If he didn't, she's taking him to the cemetery to see his and Dominique's graves."

"Good for her," Newt said. "Discussed it with the little gal 'cause none of us want to see what will happen to Baker City if Herman hires someone to burn down the town and take over. He'll destroy the place and we'll have more bodies than we got when the town was hit by those avalanches. This was a grand time, young feller. What about Kyra O'Neill and Derek Waller? Are they happy together?"

"I saw them going with Dominque MacGillicudy to the real-ty," Moises said. "They're writing offers on a house and the auto-repair place. When she said she'd contact George O'Connell and get in his schedule for the closings, Derek refused. He told her that he had his own lawyer and she'd handle it."

Mayor O'Connell whistled softly. "Good job, Pride. We need an attorney who will look after the womenfolk."

"Yes, we do." Moises waved toward the calendar behind the bar. "This project rocked. It isn't even December yet. We've got time to—"

"Time for what?" Mayor O'Connell asked.

"To do it again." Moises glanced around the room. "Let's have a real Merry Ghostmas and reform someone else on Cat O'Leary-McTavish's and Rob Hendrickson's naughty list."

"That's a great idea." Raven beamed, mischief shining in her face. "I wanna be the *Ghost of Christmas Past* this time."

"Let me think about it," Mayor O'Connell said.

"And while you do, we'll provide the musical entertainment." Zeke signaled Moises. "Help me out here. How does your song go again?"

"Like this. We wish you a Merry Ghostmas," Moises sang. By the second line, Zeke and Raven chimed in. "We wish you a Merry Ghostmas. We wish you a Merry Ghostmas and a haunted New Year—"

THE END

THANK YOU FOR READING

Did you enjoy this book?

We invite you to leave a review at your favorite book site, such as Goodreads, Amazon, Barnes & Noble, etc.

DID YOU KNOW THAT LEAVING A REVIEW...

- Helps other readers find books they may enjoy.
- Gives you a chance to let your voice be heard.
- Gives authors recognition for their hard work.
- Doesn't have to be long. A sentence or two about why you liked the book will do.

ABOUT THE AUTHOR

Josie Malone lives and works at her family business, a riding stable in Washington State. Teaching kids to ride and know about horses, she finds in many cases, she's taught three generations of families. Her life experiences span adventures from dealing cards in a casino, attending graduate school to get her master's in teaching degree, being a substitute teacher, and serving in the Army Reserve - all leading to her second career as a published author. She writes two paranormal romance series, Baker City Hearts, and Haunts, "where love is real and so are the ghosts!" and Liberty Valley Love, "where no matter what, soulmates find each other!"

Contact Josie at:
josiemaloneauthor@outlook.com

Find her on Online at:
www.josiemalone.com

Join her Newsletter:
https://sendfox.com/josiemaloneauthor

facebook.com/JosieMaloneAuthor

instagram.com/josiemaloneauthor

goodreads.com/shannonkennedy

amazon.com/Josie-Malone/e/B006HC9VMI

ALSO BY JOSIE MALONE

Baker City Hearts and Haunts

My Sweet Haunt

More Than A Spirit

Family Skeletons

Ghost of the Past

Kindred Spirits

Merry Ghostmas

Ghost Writer's Inn (coming soon!)

Liberty Valley Love

A Man's World

Cowboy Spell

The Marshal's Lady

Hero Spell

A Trail Through Time

Time In Between

Kitchen Witch (Coming Soon!)